Nan

WAKEFIELD PRESS

CW01572667

MAGPIE

Brian Matthews is a real doctor (Philosophy), Peter
Goldsworthy is a Bachelor of Medicine and Bachelor of
Surgery. Goldsworthy has won more literary awards than
Matthews, but Matthews's awards were worth more
money and prestige, allowing both to indulge in some
mutual envy. Goldsworthy's recent knee reconstruction
may allow him to play soccer again; Matthews runs for
miles and continues in Australian Rules football surro-
gately, as a commentator and passionate spectator; both
want to be professional athletes in their next lives, prefer-
ably competing against each other (it's some silly male
thing).

Peter Goldsworthy began writing poems, moved to
short stories, then to novels, then to film scripts, and
now is writing an opera libretto with the composer
Richard Mills. Brian Matthews wrote the biography of
Louisa Lawson, moved to short stories, then to sports
writing and satirical essays.

Peter Goldsworthy's next book is a novel called *Honk
If You Are Jesus*. Brian Matthews is at work on a 'baggy
novel'.

BY THE SAME AUTHORS

Peter Goldsworthy

POETRY
Readings From Ecclesiastes
This Goes With This
This Goes With That: Selected Poems

SHORT FICTION
Archipelagoes
Zooing
Bleak Rooms

NOVEL
Maestro

Brian Matthews

NON-FICTION
The Receding Wave
Louisa

SHORT FICTION
Quickening and Other Stories

ESSAYS
Oval Dreams

MAGPIE

A NOVEL BY
PETER GOLDSWORTHY
AND BRIAN MATTHEWS

WAKEFIELD PRESS

Wakefield Press
PO Box 2266
Kent Town
South Australia 5071

First published March 1992

Edited by Jane Arms
Illustrated by Geoff Kelly
Designed by Ann Wojczuk

Typeset by Midland Typesetters, Maryborough, Victoria
Printed by Australian Print Group, Maryborough, Victoria

Cataloguing-in-publication data

Matthews, Brian (Brian Ernest)
Magpie.
ISBN 1 86254 272 4.
I. Goldsworthy, Peter, 1951– II. Title.
A823.3

Promotion of this title has been assisted by the South Australian Government through
the Department for the Arts and Cultural Heritage.

PERHAPS ONE MORNING

Perhaps one morning walking through air as clear as glass
I'll turn to see a miracle performed –
a void at my shoulder, an emptiness
behind me – and reel with a drunkard's terror.

Then, as on a screen, assembled in a rush,
will come trees houses hills by the usual deceit.
But it will be too late, and I shall go on silently
among those who do not turn, guarding my secret.

Eugenio Montale

A FAX TO THE PUBLISHER

To: The Publisher, Gorgon Press
From: Professor William Barrett
Enclosed: Draft Chapter, proposed novel: 'Magpie'

Dear Mr Lovejoy

I'm forwarding a sample chapter from my new novel under separate cover. I want to repeat how grateful I am for the opportunity to publish with your firm.

Admittedly the Gorgon Press was not my first choice, but I think that fourteen rejections from other publishers is not a huge number in this business. Some of the great novels of our century had far more rejections before finding a publisher: nineteen for Philip Roth's *Catch-22*, I believe. And even more for Joyce's *Odysseus*.

The advance seems reasonable – I would have had to pay *much* more to the only other publisher who was willing to take a risk on my book.

I'm sending the first instalment of your advance by cheque at the end of the week. You do still want that cheque made out 'Cash'?

Fingers crossed for another *Catch-22* success story!

Yours sincerely

William Barrett

MAGPIE: SAMPLE CHAPTER

Bennett watched warily for the magpie. His gaze swept from the green fenceposts to the sagging barbed-wire then lifted to search the tops of trees: mournfully sighing sheoaks, spiky, swaying pines, ubiquitous sprawling stringybarks.

No magpie.

There were magpies but not *the* magpie. Bennett could pick him – her, *it* – from a hundred yards away: bigger than most of his breed; dusty where he should have been white, and greyish where he should have been black; colder and beadier of eye than his more

3

frivolous and randomly carolling comrades; long and needle-pointed of beak.

And – above all – full of malice.

Not for the first time, the magpie's salient characteristics reminded Bennett of his campus boss, Professor Harp. It might have been a little out of character for Harp to squat on a rural fencepost, or cling to a high swaying stringybark branch, but he scored highly on the rest of the check-list: dusty, greyish, cold, beady-eyed and malicious. And while his swoop was less spectacular and lacked the graceful, deadly arc of *the* magpie, it could not, on the other hand, be deflected or deterred by such a simple stratagem as wearing a white hat with the word CRETE printed on it.

Such light armour, along with his red tracksuit top and his blue-striped white shorts, protected Bennett as he jogged tensely through the danger area on a bright, mild morning in March 1992. His sockless feet, clad in his favourite though very smelly Nike Elites (with a nine millimetre build-up under the right heel and pads of folded toilet paper cushioning the blisters on various toes) hit the black bitumen with a muffled pat-pat, pat-pat, pat-pat . . .

Around and above him, birds that were not magpies whistled, screeched, flitted, chortled and piped, and magpies that were not *the* magpie fluted and warbled, practising odd, chromatic scales. On the far side of the endless fences, sturdy lambs butted their mothers in search of breakfast while the more recently born howled in panic or snuggled in sunny spots blinking sticky eyes. The sun was barely up, but already the light was golden. Wildflowers carpeted the fields, a

4

steady background hum of bees could be heard, a kind of distant, aural horizon.

None of this early morning lyricism impressed Bennett. Spring – the cruellest season – had *never* impressed him. It had always seemed a kind of con, a big spender smearing thick cosmetics over the dead land. This temporary *carnivale* of the animals – this animal *sexiness* – was all too transient for him.

Summer – the season of bushfires and drought – impressed him even less. Autumn at least was honest – everything died. Winter . . . well, winter was simply too cold. But season in, season out, Bennett dragged his reluctant body outdoors into the first light; not to be at one with Nature – numbered among whose dubious treasures was, in any case, *the* magpie – but simply so that he could, as he often put it, 'eat and drink what I bloody well like and enjoy life without worrying'. He didn't want to be fat, diabetic, rheumatoid, condemned to odd diets, gouty, infarcted, aneurysed or prematurely dead. It wasn't much to ask, as he also often said.

Not only was Bennett unimpressed by the riot of the new day on all sides, he was positively disgruntled by it. Creatures given to singing, to sitting around in trees, to sex, and to eating – meaning nothing less than the single-minded persecution of everything that moved on the sun-dappled carpet below them – were clearly unencumbered by questions of tertiary amalgamation, classes on 'method', aggressive and humourless colleagues, crumbling personal relationships, intimations of mortality and lastly, but unavoidably, the vile Professor Harp.

5

Small, petty problems? At least they partially obscured the larger: the meaning of the cosmos, the problem of evil, the question of Free Will – the whole philosophical vale of tears.

'Gloomy Boots' Bennett – 'Your Gloomship', as his wife, Jasmine, sometimes affectionately called him, plain 'Eeyore' to his colleagues – reached the crossroads that marked the outward limit of his morning run and executed a wide, slow U-turn. Without noticing, he had run safely through and out of the No-man's-land he must now re-enter for the journey home. He evacuated each nostril in a shining spray on the road, spat, cleared his throat, took several deep breaths and settled down again to his rhythm – pat-pat, pat-pat, pat-pat – reflecting as he set off that doing turns and retracing steps were excellent preparations for the professional challenges of the coming day.

How easy it had all been in the old days, he mused, almost smiling, as if the thought, instead of plaguing his mind as he jogged every morning, had occurred to him just then for the first time.

As a young man Bennett had been a teacher in a northern Victorian technical school. In those days – the last days of the fifties and the earliest and least swinging of the sixties – he was a more than competent footballer, a talented cricketer, a very ordinary but enthusiastic clarinetist in the local trad jazz band, a solid and reliable drinker, a natural raconteur and, to his considerable surprise, a gifted teacher. If there was one thing he would have improved upon, given the chance, it was his attractiveness to women, though even there, allowing for moral tentativeness and hypocrisy (his own and those the times enjoined), he could scarcely complain. So what in the name of God had convinced him that he shouldn't go on living like that? What demon (something broodingly Irish, he was sure, in his Celticly overburdened priest-ridden heritage) had sermoned him into seeking a more serious, a more profound experience of life? What idiocy had driven him back to the city in the early sixties, applying (unsuccessfully) for jobs in teachers' colleges; enrolling for MAs and MEds; competing daily, beneath a grim facade of sociability, with tense, neurotic, overworked and frustrated colleagues? Too late he realised he had forsaken the easy-going, multi-competent, classless world of a country tech for the permanently discontented, under-qualified ranks of a Melbourne suburban high school.

Bennett had given up his MA after two years and the MEd that replaced it after eighteen months. His first marriage – to Moira Kelly, the Domestic Arts teacher at Mountbank High School, where Bennett became Senior Teacher of English and History – lasted a tumultuous four and a half years and provided many a diversion for Mountbank staff and students, whose collective enjoyment of the Bennetts' numerous conflicts and eruptions in corridors and staff room may have constituted the only identifiable common ground between them.

Bennett's 'translation' – as his headmaster put it during a farewell speech – to Connman Teachers' College in Adelaide as a Lecturer in English Method proved a more lasting phenomenon. There, without ever fully grasping what exactly was meant by 'English Method', he was able to use his old classroom skills and natural teaching ability to some advantage and quickly achieved tenure and a Senior Lectureship. The MEd, on which he was still engaged at the time of applying for the post and which the interviewing panel seemed to regard as indispensable in tipping the balance in his favour, was never mentioned again, and his prompt abandonment of it, out of sheer boredom, raised not a tremor on the Academic Board or anywhere else.

As a place in which to while away the working hours of each week, Connman Teachers' College, named after some mid-western luminary or other whom Bennett had never bothered to investigate, was nowhere near as pleasant as the tech. But, for all its endless committees and recurrently proposed reforms, revamps, curricular overhauls and self-regulatory questionnaires, it was a comfortably somnolent place. Staffed almost exclusively in those days by old-hand, ex-high school teachers who regarded tenure as a miraculously inexplicable industrial agreement, and who looked upon a college lectureship as a sort of unofficial early retirement and a blessed escape from the front line of the classroom, Connman and its sister institutions were never likely to induce the stress of intellectual ferment in either staff or students. Even the revolutionary crescendo of the early seventies produced at Connman nothing lasting. The changes had been superficial only, the outward trappings of revolution: an intensification of committee work to absorb student participation; increased frequency of think-tanks planning 'total structural overhaul'; group gropes for staff solidarity and communication effectiveness;

and all-in barbecues at which bra-less young women shed their blouses and tank-tops in the heat of the night, temporarily convincing their male tutors and lecturers that even the miracle of tenure and the certainty of promotion were less important than true human togetherness and love.

Bennett glared with loathing at a Blue Heeler barking frenziedly at him from a nearby dairy and ignored the farmer's cheery wave. The familiar college scenes and phrases jogged as always through his head to the rhythm of his dogged feet.

It was so bloody unfair. He had survived Connman's numerous metamorphoses and crises throughout the seventies, submitted himself to a truly immobilising, concentrated diet of bullshit from its constantly changing leadership, endured the machinations and lobbyings of droves of self-serving tacticians and hatchet people ready at any given moment to launch the next coup – the keen and continual anticipation of which they mistook for intellectual activity.

Then, at the age of forty-eight, just when he was at least within sight of a golden handshake and freedom, Connman had amalgamated.

'Amalgamation' – that dread word. The process took a few frenetic months and was carried out with blinding haste for reasons that suited the different but consistently Machiavellian intentions of both the college and the nearby university. As Bennett remembered it – and he remembered it every morning, pat-pat, pat-pat, pat-pat – it seemed that one day he was a Senior Lecturer at Connman College (in something now called Dynamics of Communications but actually indistinguishable from the more simply named but equally inscrutable English Method), bored witless but within sight of escape; and the *next* day he was Lecturer (yes, a mere lecturer again) in 'The Literature of the English Wars' at the Flanders Fields University of the South Pacific, a hybrid institution temporarily distributed through what used to be known as Flinders University but due for transfer *in toto* to new decentralised premises at Woomera.

The whole enterprise was heavily underwritten by the Returned Servicemen's League and the Australian Army High Command which, aggrieved at what it saw as its downgrading when Duntroon Army College was subsumed by the Defence Force Academy in Canberra, had been looking for an opportunity to refurbish its institutional image. Hence the name of the university. *And* the endowed professorial chairs honouring various branches of the military, including the 15th Royal Australian Artillery Regiment Chair of Music; the Signals Corps Chair in Semiotics; the 3rd Field Kitchen's Chair of Women's Studies and Gender Theory; the 101st Airborne Division Chair in Philosophy; the CIA Chair in Latin American History; the 10th Amphibious Assault Battalion Chair of Littoral Biology; the Regiment of Military Police Chair of Psychology; a newly established RSL Chair of Migrant and Multicultural Issues; and many others still in the pipeline – or down the barrel. Which meant that, among innumerable other loathsome and intolerable obscenities (including the rapid evaporation of his golden handshake), Bennett was now working for Harp, the newly appointed incumbent of the newly formed ASIO Chair of English Literature.

Always at this point of his ruminations, through adrenalin and anger, Bennett found himself unconsciously running faster. He began flipping through the List of Required Reading for the coming semester: *The Spy Who Came In From The Cold.*, *The Spy Who Loved Me*, *Spy vs Spy* . . . This day, though, his acceleration had scarcely begun when there was a rush of air and a deafening crack at the base of his neck. His hat flew off and fell, CRETE up, on the bitumen, as he reeled forward knowing he had been shot. Knowing it for an instant, that is, before returning reason revealed the true cause.

'You fucking bastard,' he shouted at the magpie, 'you fucking creepy shitty little, I'll fucking rip you to shreds, you fucking amalgamating little up-jumped fucking turd. I'll . . .'

His voice trailed into silence. The magpie, task fulfilled, sat majestically on a stobie pole and looked down on him. Other magpies, other birds, warbled and lilted. Ewes called their lambs, lambs complained in reply; flowers consented to bees; a kookaburra gurgled into uproarious laughter.

Bennett picked up his hat and jammed it onto his head. CRETE, it said.

Slowly and reluctantly picking up his rhythm, he ran on: pat-pat, pat-pat, pat-pat, fuck-fuck, fuck-fuck, fuck-fuck . . .

III

A FAX TO THE AUTHOR

To: Professor William Barrett
From: Michael Lovejoy, Publisher, Gorgon Press

Dear Professor

Thanks for the cheque.

Good news: chapter one of your novel has been typeset. I'm returning the galleys for you to proof-read.

It looked pretty good to me. We have recently employed a new typesetter, but I've been over his work on your chapter personally and, apart from one or two typos, it brushed up fairly well.

Unfortunately, paper costs have escalated in recent weeks. To set the next chapter I will need a ten per cent increase in your next payment. As I explained before, this was *exactly* the reason I thought we were better off without signing a contract. It gives us both a lot more flexibility.

If it was just up to me I would overlook the matter – small change, really – but others depend on me.

Of course, if costs go *down* in the next few months, this also will be taken into account.

Yours in literature

Lovejoy

IV

GALLEY PROOFS

CHAPTER ONE
MAGPIE, BY WILLIAM BARRETT

The air was murky in the dawn light.

John watched warily for the magpie through the kitchen window. Somewhere out there it was waiting for him to emerge for his morning jog. Perhaps it was even watching him now.

Summoned by the whistling of the kettle, he turned away and mixed his first coffee for the day. Sipping, he began leafing through the weekend papers. An article on 'tiger widows' in Bengal caught his eye; he read of whole villages of widows whose menfolk had been torn apart by maneaters as they foraged in the surrounding forests for firewood.

Interestingly – *very* interestingly – no attacks had been recorded from the front or side of the victims: all had been from the rear, the tigers preferring to stalk and attack unseen.

John lifted his eyes from the paper and gazed through the window into the blue of the morning once again. Magpies and tigers? Was the comparison too ludicrous? Not entirely, perhaps. He knew from experience that if he watched the bird as he jogged, if he ran beneath the trees with an upturned face, it would never attack.

The idea of Jasmine as a 'magpie-widow' momentarily diverted him. He imagined her at his funeral: distraught, guilty, trying to explain how she had failed to take his obsession with the magpie seriously.

He read on. The Bengali woodcutters had taken to wearing face-masks attached to the backs of their heads. With this innovation the number of deaths had declined to almost nil. The tigers did not like being 'watched'.

'Where's my CRETE hat?' he warbled to Jasmine through a mouthful of coffee, then remembered that she had walked out on him three nights before.

He rose from the table, poured out the dregs and slipped the cup into the dishwasher. He found the hat under his tracksuit, in a wet mound on the floor in the bathroom. Back in the kitchen, he scrabbled through the oddments drawer until he found a thick felt-tip texta, then spread the hat across the table and began to draw: two eyes, a nose, a fierce, toothy mouth.

Smiling, he pulled on his tracksuit, laced his

running shoes, and jammed the hat on his head.

Outside, the day was perfect, the sun low but already warm, the birds mucking about noisily in their trees. The magpie was nowhere in sight, and as John jogged he began to suspect that he would never see the bird again.

His feeling of relief was immense: the anxiety had gone, and with it all the other trivial anxieties that it had called up every morning as he had jogged: the whole domino-chain of pseudo-problems with work, Professor Harp, his career to date, possible golden handshakes, home, even his relationship with Jasmine.

He felt somehow cleansed, full of life, free of worry for the first time in years. Suddenly he didn't give a stuff about the problems that waited at Flanders Fields. It was time for a complete change in direction. Enough of all this teaching, enough of committees, to hell with tenure! He felt an urge to do something useful, something perhaps with his hands; he vaguely remembered he'd been good with his hands as a kid.

How fine it must be to work with the hands, he thought, to actually see at the end of the day what you had achieved, perhaps even feel what you had achieved.

He remembered woodwork classes at high school, years before, how much he had enjoyed them. Perhaps there might be an opening somewhere in carpentry. His father-in-law was a carpenter, perhaps he could help. He U-turned at the half-point of his run, and headed back eagerly towards the house.

First, of course, he would ring Jasmine and tell her of his success with the magpie. And of his decision. He knew she would be pleased. He spent too much time brooding, she often told him. Too much time thinking, plotting, dreaming.

She was probably at her parents. He flipped through the phone-book, looking for the name: *Winters*. Strange that after all these years he had never actually memorised the number – but of course he had tried to ring it as little as possible, back in the old days. *White*. He ran his finger down the columns. *Witherspoon, Wittgenstein* . . .

He paused, briefly, at this last entry. The name seemed familiar, but he couldn't quite place it.

Obviously it wasn't important. He continued flipping through the pages, happily, looking for his wife, and his father-in-law, the carpenter: flip-flip, flip-flip, flip-flip . . .

A LETTER TO THE PUBLISHER

The Publisher
Gorgon Press
Poseidon Road, Kent Town

Dear Mr Lovejoy

I refer to galley proofs of Chapter One of my novel
(provisional title: 'Magpie'), which I recently received.

This chapter, as I originally designed it, introduced
the main protagonist, Bennett, who, as the book opens,

is taking his customary morning jog and is worrying about a magpie that has been persistently attacking him. This becomes the framework for a reverie in which we discover various aspects of Bennett's character, his background and his present plight. (For example, for various reasons which I needn't go into at the moment, I have *equipped* Bennett, so to speak, with a rather standard 'past' – a sort of kit, which could, and indeed does, apply to any number of people of that particular generation, especially those who, for whatever good or bad or random reasons, entered the teaching profession in the late fifties or early sixties. It is this 'past', among other things, that he reviews as he jogs along.)

I have gone into some detail here because I want to be sure that you remember the main thrust of the chapter in view of what has transpired. You claim to detect only a few 'typos' in the galleys. I can only assume you have not read my original, because I was flabbergasted to find that, apart from the first and last sentences, the chapter in proof bears only a highly tendentious relationship to the one I originally sent you.

Please do me the courtesy of comparing the two again. You will immediately see that the author, whoever he or she is, has taken my character and his situation and simply redrawn, renamed and *co-opted* him, to produce a totally different ambience while retaining some general outlines and even some details (the hat with CRETE printed on it, for instance, and certain rhythms produced by repetitions in the prose).

I trust that you recognise, as I do, that what we have

here is a case of piracy or perhaps, more accurately, *hijack*.

My questions are simple: what the hell is going on? And what are you going to do about it?

Yours sincerely

(Prof.) William Barrett

cc Amanda Pocock
Pocock & Malley Inc., Literary Agents

VI

AN APOLOGY FROM THE TYPESETTER

Dear Professor Barrett

Okay, I did it. I admit it. *I* chopped down your precious cherry tree. All by myself.

You may be pleased to know that I have lost my job as a typesetter with Gorgon Press as a result.

I write to tell you that I am *not* ashamed of tampering with your manuscript and, despite what you say in your letter to my former employer, I am not afraid to tell you so to your face. I even dared hope that you would be grateful for my modest improvements.

Surely the alleged 'piracy' could be seen merely as another component of the editorial process. Most of the so-called 'Great' novels have been assisted enormously by editors. In some cases whole chapters have been deleted, or written, or even 'hijacked' by them. And these, I repeat, are 'Great' novels. Why should your anything-but-great effort be sacrosanct?

Okay, the loss of my job is not the end of the world. It wasn't much of a job. I see myself as a *writer*, not a typesetter. The typesetting job was a temporary position only – donkey work, to some extent – until I made my own name as a writer.

Strangely enough, you got me started. Yes, you. You may remember me: John O'Hare – the same John O'Hare who took English as a major at your college. I was in your Autobiography class. Remember how I was always sitting in the front row of your lectures, by myself? (It fascinated me that the rest of the sheep would never venture into the front row of a lecture theatre.) It was me who used to ask all those questions. Surely you remember? Is fiction just a species of autobiography? was my favourite. Or why bother making up stories when what you are really doing is writing disguised autobiography, or trying to find some order, or pattern, in your experiences – isn't writing so-called fiction all a bit silly, a bit twee?

Despite my gratitude for your lectures – and answers! – and my enjoyment of some of your previous short stories, I feel that *this* novel (the novel I have tampered with) is not your best work. Surely we've read too many academic spoofs of the David Lodge, Kingsley Amis, Tom Sharpe genre. I don't object to the milieu. Some of the finest writing is restricted in content, and I don't hold that a university is any less 'real' an environment in which to set a novel than is a provincial French city, say, or the suburb of Bloomsbury, or a penal colony. No, it's more than that – something to do with tone, with stereotyped academic anti-heroes, and with a sort of prurient, dated approach to the opposite gender.

Above all, as I read I felt I could predict the entire course of the novel after only a few paragraphs. Sitting at my typesetter's screen I determined to set it on a more unpredictable path.

Difficult to believe? Let me try to second-guess you! I'll set forth here a rough precis of the events of your novel as I see them unfolding. (You will realise, of course, that I had only typeset the first chapter before being sacked, and the rest has still not arrived at the publishers.)

In brief, the following cast of characters seems obligatory:

1. A corduroyed, slightly unworldly, but always lustful, hero.

2. His wife, gone to pottery classes. Or just gone.

3a. At least one female student, decked out in the usual paraphernalia of middle-aged male fantasy and eager to maximise her assessment marks.

3b. Alternatively, a female soul-mate, or intellectual companion, of more mature years, who 'understands' our hero – perhaps a fellow staff-member, perhaps his wife's best friend.

4. A Machiavellian academic and/or sexual competitor.

5. At least one tweed-clad, pipe-smoking, elder academic continually falling asleep after losing track of arguments in faculty meetings.

6. A butch-cropped, overalls-clad, radical lesbian-marxist-anarchist – or whatever combination of 'ists' terrifies most our thinly disguised middle-aged author-protagonist.

Have I missed any of the tired roles? I'm sure you know of more.

As for plot: predictions here are even easier.

1. Dissatisfactions at home of a my-wife-doesn't-understand-me nature.

2. Conflicts with colleagues at staff meetings.

3. Sexual dalliance with female student, perhaps on his desk.

4. Exposed and/or caught at it by butch feminist.

5. Resolution at home of the all-is-forgiven variety.

Of course, you will have worked a conference in there somewhere, a chance for some cheap laughs at the expense of post-neo-structuralist-marxism, or whatever other straw figures can be set up and knocked down. The conference will also provide opportunities for further sexual dalliances with sexual fantasy figures of the type more often seen in girlie-magazine centrefolds than met on campuses.

Have I said enough? These stories are a dollar a dozen. Do we need more? Or is it – I don't mean to pry – that this is, in fact, the story of your own life? If so, you would be far more honest to set the novel in the first person, Professor. To come clean! To write – I still remember those classes – autobiography! And I'm sure it would give the story a greater sense of immediacy, a sense of being real.

Please believe me, I bear no personal grudge. I write this – I hope not too patronisingly – for your own good. You are better than this.

Yours faithfully

John Henry O'Hare

A LETTER FROM A LAWYER

The Publisher
Gorgon Press
Poseidon Road, Kent Town

Dear Sir or Madam

We are in receipt of a letter and various enclosures from our client Professor William Barrett with respect to an alleged trespass upon and partial abduction of certain fictional materials of his design and creation provisionally known as 'Magpie'.

On behalf of our client, we wish to emphasise

(a) that the copyright of 'Magpie' and all fictions subsequent upon, related to, substantially about or derivative, imitative or subsumptive of the said 'Magpie' (all of which to be known hereinafter, simply, as 'the aforesaid work in question') is vested in our client;

(b) that the milieu of the work in question (viz. Adelaide suburban middle-class life) is rightly his province and that the law of trespass dictates that the area of Greater Adelaide (a triangle roughly circumscribed by St Vincent's Gulf, Gawler River and the nearer foothills of Mount Lofty Ranges) should not be entered fictionally by any other writer without his explicit written consent. His rights in this matter are based on his several published works of fiction and non-fiction set in the area herein described and delineated;

(c) that the privacy of our client is involved in the case of certain specific details of the work in question (viz. a white hat with the word 'Crete' printed on it, which our client personally bought in Crete and which remains in his possession; and a large magpie [White-backed Magpie, *Gymnorhina hypoleuca* SE New South Wales, Victoria, southern South Australia, Tasmania] which, consistent with the extreme territoriality of the species, inhabits an area of parkland adjacent to our client's dwelling). Reference to these in fictions by other hands represents an invasion of our client's privacy and could be punishable at law.

Further clarifications and details are available

should either you or your former employee, Mr John Henry O'Hare, require them. We trust, however, that for the time being the substance of this letter will dispel any doubts or misapprehensions that may have governed Mr O'Hare's unfortunate recent trespass and that he will see the wisdom of taking no further action of the type that precipitated our client's legitimate concern.

Yours sincerely

Alaric J. Parry

Ingrid Kirsten Thrusst and Alaric J. Parry
Barristers and Solicitors
Barton Place
North Adelaide

VIII

ANOTHER LETTER FROM
ANOTHER LAWYER

Mell and Micawber, Barristers and Solicitors
Grote Street
To: The Publisher
Gorgon Press

Dear Sir or Madam

We act under instructions from an author, recently employed as a typesetter at your firm, whose attention has been drawn to the manuscript of a novel, which it is believed you intend to publish shortly. There are two immediate legal issues involved: our client's wrongful dismissal and the threat of action from your contracted author against him for an alleged hijacking of the manuscript.

We feel that both are minor issues, subsumed by a larger one. Our client intends to apply for custody of the central character and several other minor characters and animals – specifically, a magpie, *Gymnorhina hypoleuca* – in the aforementioned manuscript.

Before applying for an injunction to prevent publication, our client instructs us to negotiate with you the possibility of less divisive alternatives.

A close reading of the text has forced our client to the belief that your contracted author is not the right choice to continue the project. We would suggest that both you and your contracted author seek legal advice on this matter from a solicitor as early as possible. The case is without precedent in the world of letters, but our client feels confident he can prove that:

(a) the fictional characters in the manuscript, like all fictional characters, have certain inalienable rights, hitherto ill-defined; and

(b) your contracted author has infringed seriously on these rights during his 'stewardship' of the characters.

We have advised our client that precedents can possibly be found in the field of child welfare, and that while your contracted author may feel that he has 'invented' his charges, and that they are therefore to some extent his – and your – 'property', the same duties of parenthood or guardianship apply.

Our client can easily prove, by quotations from reviews, and calling noted expert witnesses, that readers relate to fictional characters at least to some extent in the same manner that they relate to 'real' people, and judge them likewise. Moreover, the final moral intention of literature (see Pater *vs* Arnold, and Leavis *vs* Lawrence) dictates that certain conventions in the treatment of characters must be adhered to.

This is not to suggest, simplistically, that the 'good guys' must always win, or that evil must finally be punished, but more fundamentally that certain common modes and conventions of discourse must be observed between writer and reader.

Our client is not totally opposed to what he would characterise as the academic parody that your contracted author intends, through his characters, in the context of a 'University Novel'. Our client does feel, however, that those characters would live a far more satisfying and fulfilling life within the conventions of so-called realist fiction than those of parody.

Our client asks, properly in our view, Who wants to be a cartoon character?

Our client is prepared to present various works of his own in court to demonstrate the nature of his intended foster care. His fictional world is one of familiar objects rooted in particular time and place. Time follows a chronological pattern, distances remain fixed, and metric. Characters in his custody speak succinct, individually tailored speech. Most of them – like most people everywhere – have never been near a university.

On examining the previous works of your contracted author we feel that too many of the characters speak in the manner of the author himself, that they cannot be distinguished from each other, that your contracted author is in effect putting words into their collective mouth.

His garbage-collectors, for instance, seem fully acquainted with the thought of (say) Wittgenstein; his cleaning ladies can – and therefore invariably do – quote slabs from Borges or Joyce; even his fictional children worry more over the problem of good and evil than over their spelling and sums.

Our client would put these people back where they belong: behind a truck, or a mop, or learning the three Rs. He asserts that they are not ready for fancy ideas, that such thoughts can only make them unhappy and discontented with their lot. If they genuinely wish to become acquainted with them, they should proceed through a course of normal studies, in Adult Education perhaps, and in linear chronological sequence.

It is the view of our client that too much knowledge, too quickly, can be dangerous.

Interior monologue is kept to a minimum in our client's own world. He feels that fictional characters have a right to a certain amount of privacy, that their deepest thoughts should not be eavesdropped upon, even by their alleged creator, and that only those thoughts directly relevant to the plot should be introduced into it.

Our client hopes that a settlement can be reached out of court, in an amicable manner, and that you will understand that the final decision must be in the interests of the characters themselves, and that the interests of both authors must be secondary.

He is prepared to allow your client continued interim custody of the characters until a judgment can be obtained from a suitably appointed court – perhaps the Family Court.

It would be best, however, if all communication between the two authors was through their legal advisors at this stage.

Yours faithfully

Ian Micawber

IX

YET ANOTHER LETTER TO THE PUBLISHER

Lovejoy – I'll keep this short. Perhaps I should ask you to forgive this brief scrawl on the back of an envelope, but I owe you nothing. As I'm sure you'll agree, any forgiving will be from my side.

Perhaps we won't find ourselves immersed in any deeper shit if you actually *read* my manuscript this time.

As far as payment for further typesetting goes, I am prepared to forward the next instalment on receipt of an acceptable setting of my second chapter, which please find enclosed – Barrett.

ANOTHER SAMPLE CHAPTER

CHAPTER TWO
(FINALLY)

Attention: The Publisher, Gorgon Press
From: Professor William Barrett
Contents: Sample Chapter 2, from MS 'Magpie'

Shambling round the kitchen in his sweaty running
gear, Bennett made coffee and scraped spots of green
mould from the two crumpets which seemed to rep-
resent the only chance of breakfast.

'Fucking Harp,' he muttered, randomly.

His voice echoed in the empty kitchen and died
away in the adjoining empty sitting room and empty

hallway. It was Jasmine's pre-menstrual week and, goaded beyond her temporarily fragile endurance, she had walked out on his gloomy silences two nights before amid a hail of breaking crockery.

Past experience suggested it would be three or four days before she reappeared so he decided to forget about the domestic cleaning that shame forced him to carry out in preparation for the arrival of the cleaning lady. It could wait till later. As for Jasmine, when she came back it would be only to resume what had become their obsessional discussion about Woomera: that Bennett would *have* to go and that Jasmine refused to.

Bennett sighed. He felt like a character in a novel. Nothing he did, said, thought of, or planned seemed to have any relevance to or imply any control over what actually happened to him. Whatever the plot was, he was growing tired of it. Did heroes – no, *anti*-heroes – break out of their plots? Probably not. If only he'd stayed at the tech.

Having showered and shaved, he cast a cold eye over what he sometimes referred to as his 'wardrobe', an assortment of outdated sports coats and trousers hanging on a moveable frame in one corner of the bedroom.

'Which particular ensemble shall I favour today?' he asked aloud in the musing voice of one genuinely considering his options. 'Perhaps the corduroy and . . . let me see, that goes with the corduroy. And the . . . corduroy.' An uninformed onlooker would never have realised that the assortment of cords were what he wore to work every day.

Bennett claimed to have no interest in fashion but in fact rather liked the slightly unworldly yet incipiently virile – perhaps even lustful – image that *this* fashion seemed to endow, a no doubt erroneous impression that was probably the legacy of the innumerable fictions he had read about academe. This particular morning, though, as his parody of sartorial choice neared its predictable conclusion, he paused in mid-selection. He released the corduroy coat with the leather elbow patches on its wire hanger, and it swung back into the anonymity of the rack; the corduroy trousers hung expectant but untouched.

With a feeling of revolutionary recalcitrance – as if he were defying some phantom prescription with which he was confidently expected to conform – Bennett took down his new suit.

Jasmine had urged it on him in an exclusive Mens' Wear boutique only a few months earlier, a place in which he had been a little surprised to find himself, mid-Saturday morning. The suit was easily the most upmarket article of clothing he owned. To it he added a clean pink shirt (the front and collar of which he ironed cursorily) and a subtly matching tie. The effect – even allowing for the dissonance of desert boots, which couldn't be helped because his black shoes were full of holes – was rather stunning. And . . . transforming.

Bennett felt absurdly liberated, as if he had won a small victory. But against whom? Against what?

The questions made him uneasy; he dismissed them. Resplendent in his new ensemble, he picked up his bag, failed to find his car keys, circled the kitchen, found them on the floor next to two empty red wine bottles and walked out slamming the door hard behind him.

The house, on its several secluded bushy acres, gleamed in the sun. A rooster crowed and parrots brawled in a dead gumtree.

'Fuck,' Bennett would normally have muttered, gloomily, at this point. But his mood had somehow altered. He felt almost exhilarated. But about what? Certainly not the prospect of another day at Connman/Flanders. Cheerfully dismissing this dilemma, strangely impervious to it, he tossed his bag in the back seat of his car, folded his aching jogger's body behind the wheel, and began the long drive down to the city on the plain.

At half past eight, having reached the relative safety of his office, Bennett took a few deep breaths, made a cup of instant coffee and put his feet up on the desk.

Another Flanders Fields day was about to start, yet he still felt free of the usual dread that filled him as he contemplated a day's horrific possibilities. What had happened? Nothing! Nothing especially good, at any rate. He had neither smoked nor sniffed nor swallowed nor injected any known controlled substance. Was it perhaps his suit that was making the difference?

This absence of depression worried him – even depressed him a little – and he tried to make a mental inventory of the impending events that *ought* to be filling him with gloom.

First: there were to be individual staff interviews

that morning at which Harp would be 'apportioning certain responsibilities'. Bennett's time-slot was nine o'clock, and he was bound to cop some ghastly, unimaginably witless task that he would not understand and that everyone, including Harp, would have forgotten about by the time he bungled his way through it.

Second: the new university's crass bid for corporate money meant that a stream of what Harp called 'ontraprenoors' would shuttle endlessly through various academic meetings and gatherings giving 'presentations'.

One of these was to take place during lunchtime.

Third: as part of a now well-established ritual in what they liked to refer to as their 'relationship', Bennett would have to ring Jasmine and negotiate her return.

He very much wanted her to come back, but the process was wearying, necessitating the trading of niceties, the balancing of veiled insults and the strenuous batting back and forth of culpabilities.

Fourth: when he reached home again after the hard day that was shaping up, he would have to clean the house in preparation for the arrival the following morning of Mrs Van Ness, his cleaning lady.

Mrs Van Ness (whom Bennett secretly referred to as 'The Monster') was a mature-age student at Flanders Fields and had long since made it clear that she expected to clean only a *clean* house.

They might have got on if she'd been a more normal mature-age student, decked out in the usual paraphernalia of middle-aged male fantasy and desperate to maximise her marks. But, no, Mrs Van Ness favoured austere, Thatcherite twin sets; was of formidable if somewhat unfocused intellect; had very little time for any of her fellow humans but especially not for men; quoted Wittgenstein with authority; and, far from inflaming Bennett's libidinous potential, terrified him so thoroughly that he could scarcely string a sentence together in her presence.

All in all, a truly awful though thoroughly typical day looming. Yet, cautiously he had to admit it, Bennett felt not at all oppressed. Was he coming down with something?

He broke wind noisily and waited for the knock on the door and the colleague bursting in, which such indiscretions always seemed to induce, especially if his office air had become offensively polluted.

No one came. All was quiet.

Bennett looked around him at the familiar shelves, the desk and chairs, the battered, lidless electric jug in which he boiled water for his coffee . . .

A strange and utterly inexplicable elation seized him. Perhaps I'm having an epiphany, he thought.

'More likely a stroke,' he added aloud. 'A Transient Ischaemic Attack,' he said sententiously.

(He'd learned this term from a book Jasmine's firm had recently published: *Enjoying Your First Stroke* . It was one in a self-help series, which included *Do-It-Yourself Sex-Change, Creative Abortion and Your Star-Sign* and *Eating for Orgasm*.)

With the air of a man who had decided to run with his luck, he picked up the phone and dialled Jasmine's office number.

'Hi there!' her voice said brightly. 'You have reached the number for Medusa Publishing. There is no one available to take your call at the moment, but please, *please* do not hang up. We *want* to take your call, we are avid to hear your voice. If you will leave your name, number and a message if you wish, either Trudy or Dale or myself will get back to you as soon as possible. Please leave a message after the tone, we really *want* to hear from you. Have a nice day . . . '

Bennett waited patiently through all this, amused for once at its bright, chatty, almost Californian tone. Such cheerful early morning feel-goodness usually drove him even deeper into despair. For the same reason he was unable to visit her in her workplace, it always left him depressed: Dale, Jasmine's employer (and, Bennett suspected, a Californian although he always claimed to be a New Yorker), had cute signs and Very Funny messages plastered up on every wall: *Smile!, Think!, You-Don't-Have-To-Be-Crazy-To-Work-Here-But-It-Sure-Helps.*

'This is the Flanders Fields University Answering Machine answering your answering machine,' he said after the Beep. 'All is forgiven. Come home tonight and learn something to your advantage. Note that as a genre the Answering Machine Message is new and a difficult medium for young writers to grapple with. Yours, in particular, smacks of juvenilia. I am planning an introductory course in the genre next semester and would be happy to advise on replacing your message with something more original, more durable and essential.' He paused. 'Beep,' he added, for maximum verisimilitude.

He put the phone down and stood for a moment gazing out the window at the distant and dispassionate blue of St Vincent's Gulf. Then, with an exaggerated spasm of energy, he picked up a folder marked 'Professor Harp – Meetings' and busily swapped its contents – five or six A-4 sheets covered in doodles – for clean pages.

Glancing at his watch, he began to plan what he saw as a 'strategic' entry to Harp's office: for this morning, he decided on a breezy knock/enter/ immediately-comment-on-the-weather/sit-down-before-being-asked-to/ routine, a style of entry which, as he well knew, Harp detested.

Poised to begin this routine, he noticed that he still felt absurdly cheerful, the mind-altering properties of his new suit apparently not yet wearing off, the clothes somehow *making* the man, or at least altering his character.

Rushing to Harp's office in a parody of dutiful breathlessness, Bennett executed his planned entry, eliciting from the pudding-like Harp visage a wince.

Bennett leaned forward attentively in his chair with a Faber-Castell Fluorescent Textliner (mistakenly snatched up at the last minute instead of his Ball Pentall/Medium) poised above the pages of his Reding Spiral Shorthand 200-page notepad – all relics of the defunct Connman College, where state-of-the-art stationery had always been available in prolific and unsupervised amounts.

'Yes, a really beautiful morning,' Bennett added to

his already lengthy, if slightly gasping, encomium on the weather. 'Too good to work, eh Prof!'

Bennett laughed with immoderate gusto, slapped his knee and repeated the sentence. Like most people with undeserved titles, Harp was punctilious about correct address and hated the abbreviation – as Bennett well knew.

'You will be pleased to know,' Harp said, breaking frostily into yet another effusion from Bennett about the sunshine and the open air, 'that I have obtained permission from the Acting Dean to establish a course entitled "Refugee Literature: The Contribution of Military Dictatorships to Australian Multiculturalism". You see the point, of course. The study will deal with the writing of those who have been driven to our shores by military oppression in their own country. The boat people, for example, should perhaps be grateful to their oppressors for the opportunity to begin a new life . . . '

Harp waved a silencing arm, mistaking Bennett's embarrassed squirm for incipient protest.

' . . . we can discuss the fine detail at the appropriate time. I mention the matter now in order to say that I would like you, Dr Bennett, to take charge of a multi-cultural presentation to be given to the whole faculty as a basis for heightened awareness of the issues and informed discussion of our plans in that regard.'

Bennett smiled and nodded. He'd been expecting something like this. And, anyway, he still felt gen-uinely cheerful beneath the hearty facade. Not only that, but he had experienced, during Harp's descrip-tion of the new course, a sudden, totally irrational yet irresistibly persuasive, conviction that he need not worry; that Harp, Woomera and the whole mad system were irrelevant; that forces more powerful than any of them could imagine or conceive of were making claims on all of them and that, when everything was settled either by powerplay or negotiation, none of them would be going to Woomera, or, perhaps, anywhere.

It gave him some satisfaction to decide that his uncharacteristic cheerfulness might actually proceed from wholly apocalyptic and potentially nihilistic intuitions.

'Dr Bennett?'

He realised he must have been looking rather glazed. Harp's little eyes were strobing out at him from behind the thick glasses.

'Absolutely, Prof. Leave it all to me. Multicultural. Presentation. Just like SBS, eh!'

Bennett stood, still jabbering away about SBS and subtitles and ethnic applicability till he was sure Harp had not the slightest idea what he was talking about. Then, with a quick word of farewell and another burst on the glorious weather, he was rocketing out into the corridor where he bumped heavily into Dr Carrington, nearly knocking his colleague over.

'Bloody hell, Bennett, what are you . . . '

Bennett took his colleague's arm and moved away from Harp's office, saying loudly as he did so, 'Ah, Dr Carrington, I wanted to talk to you about an idea Professor Harp and I are working on – multicultural actually. You may want to . . . '

A POLITE REQUEST FROM THE
PUBLISHER

Dear Professor Barrett

Thank you very much for chapter 2 of your charming novel, which I have read with great interest and enthusiasm.

You will be pleased to learn that we have dismissed the typesetter – O'Hare – who caused so much trouble with your earlier chapter, not without a scene, I might add, and threats from O'Hare of legal action.

Of course I hold myself completely responsible – inadequate supervision as you so rightly pointed out.

That said, I wonder if I could make a few small suggestions as to how we might, not improve, but perhaps *enhance* your excellent work.

It's trite but true to say that televison has destroyed the attention span of the new generation of readers: that the works of a Tolstoy, a Proust – or even a Barrett – might have moved beyond the intellectual reach of the 'baby-boomers'.

I feel your own novel is moving in the direction of this, and feel I must, in fairness, point this out, that, in short, the work is in danger of bogging down. If you think you cannot compromise your work by 'peppering' it up a little – adding a little tabasco – think of the example of Shakespeare who was not averse to introducing scenes of graphic violence, or of Dickens who wrote, 'When in doubt, kill a baby.'

'When in doubt, bring in a man with a gun,' as Raymond Chandler said, topping them all.

I find, myself, that a little Love Interest is sometimes the best way to go.

I thought I would fly these thoughts past you, the views of one reader, only, of course, which you can take or leave.

I enclose an invoice for your next payment. Perhaps we could negotiate a deduction for every baby killed, or any attractive female character that you might like to introduce.

Yours respectfully

Michael Lovejoy

CHAPTER THREE
A LITTLE TABASCO

Bennett walked across the leafy main quadrangle with his colleague Dr Carrington – Dr *Amanda* Carrington.

She was his one real friend in the department. On their middle-aged shoulders the sun flung spangles, dancing coins.

'It's simply unbelievable,' Amanda was saying.

Her chiselled, high cheek-bones caught and discarded the bright light as she strolled along; her blonde hair rose and fell with the movement. She was wearing a tight scabbard of blue jeans, a white blouse and a smart black top-coat of some shiny-looking material.

She looked, as always in Bennett's view, sensational. She had been one of the most outstanding academics in the pre-amalgamation university and her position at Flanders Fields, where neither intelligence nor scholarship counted as highly as 'ontraprenoorial' skills, would have been intolerable had she been doomed to stay. But Bennett knew (the only one she'd so far told) that Amanda had cracked an Associate-Professorship in a real university in the east.

Her husband, a well-known fiction writer, had already left to research the housing possibilities; Amanda would be giving a month's notice in a day or two and following him.

' . . . unbelievable. I mean, who would have thought things could come to this?'

Bennett had finished telling her of the multicultural presentation and Harp's planned course on Refugee Literature.

'We're nothing but a . . . a fucking big business operation,' she went on. 'We've got less academic reputation than a northern suburbs high school . . . '

Bennett shrugged his resigned agreement, squinting in the bright sun. As they approached the far side of the quadrangle, they heard a musical babble of voices, much laughter and the crunch of shoes on gravel.

Round a corner came a wave of Japanese, one of the regular inspection tours prefiguring the transmutation of the site into the Nippon Centre. Cameras were aimed, lenses pointed like gunbarrels. The air filled with whirrs, clicks, chatters and whines as sprocketing film raced and unrolled like ammunition

48

belts; streaks of sunlight tracered out from angled viewfinders and shiny fittings; from the cameras of those in the shade, automatically activated flashbulbs burst in blinding volleys.

'God,' Amanda said, 'it must have been like this on the Kokoda trail.'

Bennett mimed a fatal wound, telling Amanda to leave him and save herself . . . The Japanese flowed by with much laughing and camera business.

'I'm sorry,' Amanda said. 'I shouldn't have said all that. About this place, I mean. I know you're probably stuck here, or in Woomera.'

'Well, I guess I am. But you'll be surprised to hear, Amanda, that I feel no pain. In fact I feel wildly optimistic about things generally. I have this definite feeling that I won't end up in Woomera or working for Harp. I can't explain it, but . . . '

'Good God,' she said, looking at him with affectionate surprise. 'I *am* talking to "Eeyore" Bennett, aren't I?'

Bennett attempted a donkey sort of noise, but it didn't quite come off. Amanda laughed anyway.

'Well, I hope you're right,' she said. 'I won't ask how you've come to this mystic insight.'

'No point. Can't explain it myself. Probably mid-life crisis in some new manic form.'

Shortly after, they parted, each to their own office.

Placing his fingers lightly on the inside of Amanda's ankle, Bennett ran his hand the length of her long leg to the warmth of her inner thigh. She murmured. He repeated the caress; her eyes closed, her thighs moved slightly apart. Wafting past the parts that there adjacent lay he stroked the right breast and kissed the left. She groaned and the quilt rose as her legs bent and her pelvis arched momentarily from the mattress. Amanda's manicured nails dragged exquisitely across his shoulders as Bennett kissed her parted lips, a premonitory brushing; his hand strayed down to . . .

The phone rang. Bennett abandoned his reverie, lifted his feet from the desk and, leaning forward with some difficulty, picked up the receiver. It was Harp's secretary, passing on a demand from her boss that the multicultural presentation be ready by the following day.

Bennett made some agreeable noises, and set down the receiver.

Drawing him towards her, wriggling sensuously to slide beneath him, taking his buttocks in her hot cupped hands, Amanda . . .

But the fantasy was broken: Harp had intruded. There was work to be done. Bennett rearranged himself at his desk and thought about his plan for the multicultural presentation.

'Subtitles!' he exclaimed aloud, inspiration hitting him. 'Just like SBS.'

He would knock up a few dozen sheets of cardboard on which would be written English translations of the numerous phrases in Italian, Spanish and French that he intended to use. '*Je ne parle que la Francais*,' he would say at the start to the assembled audience, then hold up the appropriate board on which would be printed: 'I speak only French.' '*O Italiano*,' he could add: up with the board saying 'Or Italian.' '*Hablo Espagnol*,' grabbing for the board saying, 'And Spanish.' '*Kursunan saypan*' another board would thank them – in phrase-book Hungarian.

Any question addressed to him in English would be answered with a brandished board 'subtitle' without regard to relevance. Few would be in a position to criticise. He intended to find the Spanish, French, Italian and other translations for a whole range of phrases: *my postilion has dropped his packet of condoms; the night air has invaded my briefs; does this train go to Vladivostok?; my whips and vaseline are missing from my room; your attendant has parked my car in the fountain; the cleaning maid has accidentally released my pet cobra; my wife has been penetrated by a bell-boy; there is a nun hanging out the carriage window and we are approaching a tunnel; I have no gun – it is my metal-studded truss which has tripped your security alarm.*

Easily amused, Bennett grinned quietly to himself and decided to celebrate a fruitful morning's work by ringing Amanda and suggesting lunch in the staff club. As he reached for the phone, he had one of those irrelevant mental visions that sometimes surface with no warning: he saw his kitchen at home – empty; the sunlight pouring through the floor-to-ceiling window; the dishes piled on the sink; the fridge switching on and off through its foolish and unremarked ritual; the electric clock blandly muttering on the wall above the dresser; the long, scrubbed top of the pine table gleaming in the morning light.

The image disintegrated as his hand wavered indecisively above the phone. Yet he found it curiously unsettling. For no apparent reason, and certainly with no available evidence that he knew of, he was suddenly convinced of a connection between his uncharacteristically elated mood of that morning, his intuition that somehow escape from present woes was imminent, and the apparently random, but extraordinarily vivid, vision of his kitchen – as it was *now* while he was away: not a memory but a vision.

Who *was* it, anyway, who had written about the kitchen table when no one was there? He prowled the bookshelves snapping books out of and back into their places with a nervous verve. Some spun from his too-quickly grasping fingers; a few exploded into a confetti of bookmarks as he thumbed futilely through; most emitted mushroom clouds of dust. None yielded an answer. Then, embarking on a second tour of the shelves, he noticed Virginia Woolf's *To the Lighthouse*. The name on the spine forced its way inside him; he knew instantly that was it. He flicked through his copy – more dust wafting – and there it was:

Whenever (Lily Briscoe) thought of his work she always saw clearly before her a large kitchen table. It was Andrew's doing. She asked him what his father's books were about. 'Subject and object and the nature of reality,' Andrew had said. And when she said Heavens, she had no notion what that meant. 'Think of a kitchen table then,' he told her, 'when you're not there.'

'Subject, object and the nature of reality,' Bennett intoned. 'Subject, object and . . . '

There was a loud knocking, the door knob rattled furiously and Guy Pertwee burst into the room.

Bennett glanced up at him with distaste. Pertwee was a member of the original, unamalgamated university, a tireless Machiavellian conspirator whose only conversation, aside from internal politics and the management, fancied or real, of power plays, concerned sexual conquest among the female students and staff. In these two fields he had mistakenly identified Bennett as both cohort and competitor.

'Just had coffee with the divine Gaylene,' Pertwee purred, spoiling the effect by puffing a little.

Bennett said nothing.

'Gaylene Hawker,' Pertwee prompted. 'Ballistics 2A.'

Pertwee collapsed into Bennett's office chair and spun around on it a couple of times. His hair was a black mane, with a matching black moustache, which he stroked continually. His undeniably handsome, muscular face (artificially tanned at all times) was just beginning the process that would result in pouchiness of cheeks and bagginess of eyes. Likewise, his superficially trim figure – always smartly and fashionably clothed – was straining here and there at buttons or seams, pushing minutely but noticeably over his belt. His whole body was in a tight, silent frenzy of marginality, just about ready to pass over into an irretrievable middle-age of spreads, sags and bulges.

'The divine Gaylene wanted some advice on an essay,' Pertwee added urbanely. 'My God, what a figure. Imagine it! Imagine what it'd be like! Which is all you'll do, Bennett my boy. Imagine. And in a week or so, I'll let you know. I'm on course to savour her – what is it the man says? ah yes – her "divine fulcrum". Incidentally, Harp has more or less promised me a

Readership if I take over the Transition to Amalgamation Committee and make it work. Which . . . ' he spun the chair through several rotations ' . . . which I will do. So . . . '

'Well, that's all very fascinating, Guy, and thanks for telling me. Why *have* you told me, by the way? What the hell do I need to know all this shit for?'

'Because Bennett, my boy, because . . . '

Pertwee stopped as if unable to remember what should come next. An expression of enlightenment crept slowly over his heavy features, and he said, 'Because I am your Machiavellian academic and sexual competitor. Not bad eh? Got that from some University Novel. Something to be learned from them, actually. Anyway, must strike a blow. If you see the divine Gaylene, try to calm her down and reassure her I'll be looking after her as soon as I'm free. With my Arrow of Desire.'

His loud laughter was cut off by the slam of the door. The spinning office chair gradually slowed to a stop – facing the wrong way. Bennett picked it up and moved it clear of the desk. He sat down, extended his legs and tried to spin, but somehow he didn't seem able to work up the momentum that Pertwee had.

'Bugger him.'

Bennett recalled Pertwee's strange and uncharacteristic words: *I am your Machiavellian academic and sexual conspirator*. Uncharacteristic, but true: Pertwee acted so completely within a role so stereotyped and so conscientiously and perhaps consciously adhered to that he almost parodied himself. No, *did* parody himself, and tried to force Bennett to conform to his – Bennett's – part in the drama: a conniving, tired lecher.

Which he did all too often, Bennett realised, at least in his mind and imagination: he would *love* to outsmart Pertwee and beat him professionally; he also devoted much time to fantasising a thorough, rapturous fuck with Gaylene Hawker. He knew he was only too ready to mark up her essays, if not from a C to an A (he had some integrity), then at least to a good B, in return for certain favours.

Yet, even as he realised this, he was also aware that these reactions felt somehow . . . foreign. To part of him at least. They seemed too much part of a routine, a formula with which, if he didn't think too much about it, he complied predictably; went through the motions. But the fact was ('in real life', he almost found himself saying) he was *not* a womaniser; and he did not care much about promotion. What on earth was happening to him? It was as if someone or something had imprisoned him in a role, a facile plot, and the graft had only partly taken – one part of him had suddenly become aware of his plight.

Bennett paced up and down the room in a frenzy of euphoric anxiety. He felt as if much was impending. That was it: things were imminent. He was living minute by minute instead of at the usual grind. He recalled his earlier morose conviction that he was a hapless character in a novel. Perhaps he'd somehow strayed *out* of role . . .

What if it was true that all life was a text, as the theorists said? (There was one in an office down the corridor, a small scurrying Francophile who seemed to want to guillotine all the old-style humanists in the department.) Then we were engaged in time-honoured roles dictated by our personalities, our employment, our education, by the Great Writer from whom the Text unfolded. That was why we chose to wear, for example, certain clothes, indeed certain *ensembles*.

Bennett laughed in triumph. Had he not that very morning deliberately resisted his true self by choosing the suit instead of his coat and cords? With abrupt resolution, as if something new and important had suddenly occurred to him, as if he were about to perform a test, he strode across the room, opened the door and looked out into the passageway.

He was not at all surprised to recognise the loose-limbed nonchalant pelvic roll of Gaylene Hawker as she strolled towards him: a woman, Pertwee had once put it, poured out of honey.

'Mr Bennett,' she breathed as she came abreast of his door. 'I wondered if we might talk. It's about my term assessment.'

And it seemed to Bennett suddenly that he was helpless before this *predictable* script, that he – and she, *all* of them – were the playthings of forces beyond their control, and that he might as well, at least for the time being, bend to those forces. 'Go with the Flow,' to use one of the expressions Jasmine had brought home from her Californian employer.

'Come in,' he said.

He glanced up and down the corridor; no one was in sight. But as he closed the door and turned towards Gaylene to 'reassess' her term grade he deliberately left the door unlocked. Part of him knew what was

coming next, and almost welcomed it – the door opening, mid-reassessment, and someone walking in on
them – probably Karyn 'Rambo' Throsby, if the plot
was as predictable as he was coming to believe.

Even as Gaylene began stroking his chest he was
watching the door – waiting, half in hope, half in res-
ignation – for that stock character to enter: a crop-
haired muscular young woman dressed in blue
bib-and-brace overalls. 'Rambo' Throsby was a member of any number of committees of Women For this
and Against that. Most particularly, and the reason
Bennett suspected that she would enter his room at
any moment, Throsby was the founder of the campus
branch of Women Against Sexual Harrassment.

'Ah Karyn,' he prepared to say. 'Come on in. Or
rather stay in, now you're in. I've been expecting you
of course. All part of the . . . of the . . . another minute
or two and you might have been too late.'

FAMILY COURT JUDGMENT

BARRETT *vs* O'HARE

The court has considered at length the various submissions offered by counsels acting for Professor William Barrett, and for Mr John O'Hare; and in addition has taken note of the submission from Gorgon Press.

Before giving judgment, the court wishes to express its deep concern over recent 'developments' in fiction, in which the entire form of the novel is treated as a plaything. The court feels that fictional characters deserve a chronological sequence of life events, not the random flashbacks and fastforwards that are increasingly common in such works, and that the brief candles of their lives need, above all, the solid foundation of a beginning, a middle and an end.

The life of a character in a short fiction, or a bit-player in longer works can be as evanescent as the life of a butterfly, but that provides no grounds for mistreatment.

The court feels that the breakdown in moral norms and mores within our society to some extent mirrors the breakdown in the art forms of society; that the dislocation in family life mimics the dislocations seen on screens and in books. Not so much in the *content* of those art forms – in violence between characters, say – as something far more fundamental: a loss of belief in the solidity of the form itself.

Taking these factors into account the court believes that the best interests of the characters in the afore-mentioned manuscript might be served by granting custody to Mr O'Hare, whom the court believes may be in a position to offer the character of 'Bennett', in particular, a better, and certainly a more useful, life.

This is not to deny that there is a place for fun and games, for academic spoofs, or even for so-called discontinuous narration, or tense-changes, or now-you-see-me-now-you-don't-type 'clever-dick' narrators. These may well have their place, and the court is prepared to grant Professor Barrett weekend access to his characters, and animals, for the purposes of such 'fun', under certain conditions.

One condition of such access is that the characters must be returned to Mr O'Hare's care each Sunday evening of the same weekend. And in the same month and year. And century. They must be returned unharmed and unchanged and of the same approximate age and size and health and mental development. They must also be returned in the same tense (the court understands that Mr O'Hare would normally use the past imperfect tense) and in the same narrative person (usually, third).

The court believes that the balance that will result from such an arrangement: viz. a life spent within the accepted conventions of realist fiction from Monday to Friday, with weekends and public holidays free for parodies, or for metafictional fun and games, reflects accepted standards of behaviour in our society, and is a fair decision, which attempts to balance the interests of all parties, but particularly those of the fictional characters, to whom the court's first duty must lie.

Declared at Adelaide, this 30th day of May, 1992.

XIV

CHAPTER FOUR
A VOID AT MY SHOULDER, AN EMPTINESS
BEHIND ME

With the door of his room locked, a hasty sandwich eaten, and a cup of Instant steaming near to hand on the desk, Bennett crouched over his portable typewriter.

Technologically, he need not have inclined so much towards the Luddite: one of the by-products of amalgamation was a cloned IBM word processor assigned to every member of staff. This prodigality had not impressed Bennett; he would have scorned the machine in any case, but his resolve was merely strengthened when, in response to his one serious attempt to operate the clone – or, as his colleague Pertwee called it with easy familiarity, the IBM, thus obscuring its second-rate lineage – it had continually urged him to ABORT, INSERT, RETRY ENTRY or JUMP. Deciding it was just his luck to get a sexually perverted word processor, Bennett had abandoned the machine; it squatted inertly in its workstation day after day, staring ahead with its large blind greenish eye.

And so Bennett crouched over his portable typewriter. A little more than an hour had passed since Gaylene Hawker had left his room, in tears, in the protective custody of 'Rambo' Throsby, the latter threatening to report him to almost everybody in the entire tertiary education sector; the former looking lofty, hurt and still poured out of honey.

Bennett was still a little shaken from the encounter – its predictability had provided no immunity. The emotions, as Hamlet said, are not skilled workers. He felt little shame and less fear, however, about it all. He was in the grip of an even greater excitement than that which had overtaken him in the arms of Gaylene Hawker.

Full revelation was close, he felt. The suit and his coat and cords had provided the first clue that things were unravelling, that the universe he inhabited seemed to be developing some fissures in the consistency of its natural laws.

Fissures also seemed to be developing in the consistency – the *continuity* – of his own personality. He pulled down a book from the shelves: Derek Parfit on the continuity of the self. The human brain can survive the loss of one whole hemisphere, Parfit wrote, and function reasonably. What, therefore, if the brain were split into its two component hemispheres, and one of these was transplanted into another, brainless, body?

Both bodies would now believe they were the original self – *both* would go on and live separate lives, go their own unique ways.

Bennett's pulse quickened again as he read on. What if, Parfit asked, after a certain period, the two hemispheres were reunited?

Bennett was close to something here, he knew it; he was close to some insight. He also felt strangely, almost dizzily, disorientated. He stared at the page in the typewriter. He felt as if he could produce an exhilarating theoretical essay if he just concentrated on the discovery that was waiting for him only a shade to his left or right. The room sang with it.

What would it be like to have various hemispheres grafted on, or taken away, different sets of memories, different ambitions, different wants plugged in . . .

Still gripped by a sense of discovery and excitement, Bennett listed these points on his notepad. He began constructing in his mind the title of his resounding essay: 'Narrative and the Nature of the Fictional Self' or 'Narrative and Fictional Identity'. That was it: 'Narrative and Fictional Identity'.

He jerked the paper from the carriage of his typewriter and wound in a fresh sheet. *Narrative and Fictional Identity*, he typed. *By* . . .

Here he paused, stymied. By whom? By . . . Bannon? Burford? Burton? A cold sweat covered his face as he struggled to remember *his own surname*. He closed his eyes and concentrated, and a name surfaced, but it was not a surname: John.

He typed the name obediently: John.

But that was absurd. You didn't sign things like that – with your given name alone. He closed his eyes again, but nothing more would come. His face paled, his heart accelerated, another cold sweat broke out across his brow, he felt a rush of nausea.

Replaying through innumerable remembered conversations, it seemed to him that no one, not even Amanda, had ever addressed him by a surname. Or if they had, that name in his memory had been utterly extinguished. Or changed, as if his memories had been fed through a Find-and-Change Utility.

He glanced angrily at his IBM.

He leapt up, pulled some books from the bookshelves, and inspected their flyleafs. *John*. He jerked opened the door of his office and stared at its nameplate: *John*. Not even the hint of a surname.

He hurried down the corridor into the Men's, splashed cold water on his clammy face, and inspected himself in the mirror. What did he look like? *Who* did he look like? The name 'Bennett' came to him from somewhere. But he didn't know why; perhaps it was just probability. Smith, Jones, Green – any of these common names would probably fit as well.

Was it in print anywhere? He didn't know. Gazing at his list, he tested himself on the other criteria. Hadn't he that very morning felt as if he was part of someone else's plot? And what *were* his childhood memories? He couldn't be sure. *He wasn't sure what they were.*

John fainted. He woke to find dusk invading the room. He collected his keys, locked up and left the building. His colleagues of course had long since departed; some of them had not ever arrived. The ill-lit corridors echoed to the crash of emptying bins, the whine of floor polishers and snatches of hooted song or shouted conversation from the enviably carefree cleaning staff – cleaning staff (he briefly allowed himself to notice) who were behaving *quintessentially* as cleaning staff, singing and clattering in the manner of stereotypes, in a way that 'real people' would never have considered for a moment.

John walked stolidly through the corridors. Two cleaning ladies hilariously discussing Wittgenstein broke off their conversation to nod as he passed.

He ignored them. He needed professional help, he needed someone to talk to.

CHAPTER FIVE
A VISIT TO THE DOCTOR

The doctor glanced up from the manila case-folder as John was ushered into his office, first patient on a busy morning. The folder contained a single sheet only, with one or two lone entries at the top of a blank page: possibly the thinnest, or healthiest, folder in his files.

'Haven't seen you for a while,' he murmured, disapprovingly.

It might have been an accusation; an accusation of good-health. For some ridiculous reason John felt a little guilty for his excellent physical condition.

The doctor peered over his half-moons: 'A regular check-up wouldn't go amiss.'

'Last time I came you were away,' John said. 'I saw a locum.'

The doctor leant back: his eyes unfocussed, dreamily: 'Ah, yes – Italy,' he murmured. 'Venice.'

'But I'm here now.' John tried to regain his attention.

'Yes, of course. I suppose you are. And so am I. What can I do for you?'

'It may sound strange . . . ' John began.

The doctor watched him, waiting. He was getting on in age; near retirement, John guessed. Knowing no one else, and seldom needing medical attention, he still travelled across town to visit the old family doctor when the occasional need arose.

He took a deep breath, and continued: 'It's my moods. I don't seem to have any control over them. Like being different people: one day I'm one person, the next day someone else.'

'We all have our little moods.'

'Maybe. I don't want to be melodramatic, but I feel like Jeckyll and Hyde. And sometimes neither. Sometimes I feel I'm . . . fading away.'

'You feel weak?'

'No, I feel I'm not real. As if, well, as if everyone had stopped thinking about me, thinking *of* me, and I was just . . . disappearing. Slowly. As if I were being written out of my own life.'

The doctor reached over and pinched him sharply on the arm.

'Ouch!'

'Real enough?'

'Of course. It's more a mental thing. Maybe I'm going looney.'

The doctor humphed: a definite, audible humph, exactly as John had often seen it written.

'You're as real as me,' he said. 'Perhaps you're working too hard?'

'Not really.'

The doctor seemed a little irritated by this disagreement. 'Then perhaps you're not working hard enough. Perhaps you should busy yourself in work.'

John said nothing, irritated himself.

'Sleeping well?' the doctor asked, as if sensing his dissatisfaction.

'Too much, if anything. And that's another thing. I'm having blackouts. Periods when I can't remember what I've been doing, where I've been. Periods when I can't remember my name.'

The doctor pushed over his case-folder, and pointed with his biro: *John*.

'Cut back on the booze,' the doctor advised. 'It's bad for your memory.'

'I'm a teetotaller,' he lied.

'Hmm,' the doctor said, and lengthened the word into a hum: a filibustering hum to give him time to think what to ask next, John suspected.

'How are things at home?' he eventually came out with.

'Not so good,' John said, and immediately regretted admitting the fact, for he could sense the doctor prick up his ears, looking for some easy cause to pin his symptoms on.

'What's the problem?'

'Jasmine and I are having difficulties,' he said. 'We're apart. Temporarily. While we sort a few things out.'

'Well,' the doctor smiled, as if enormously pleased to hear this news. 'That explains everything.'

'How does it explain everything?'

'Common enough reaction,' the answer came. 'You're on your own. Nothing to think about but yourself. We all get a bit hypochondriacal. I think you should just forget all this nonsense about a split personality. I don't want to sound rude, but you academics are all the same. You read too much. Get out more. In the real world. Busy yourself. Or take a holiday.'

He paused, and smiled again, waiting, smugly satisfied.

When John failed to take the cue, he added: 'The receptionist will have your bill. But make sure you book a time for a regular check-up.'

'Going to Italy again?' John murmured.

'Beg yours?'

Nothing, he wanted to add, but then he seemed to black out again, and when he next fully orientated himself, or could remember where he was, he was far from the surgery, driving home.

CHAPTER SIX
MEMORIES

He had wanted to tell the doctor about the memories,
too.

Or, more correctly, the lack of them.

He found, when he tried, that he could remember
very little from the past. His childhood, for instance.
He didn't seem to have any, to speak of. Or nothing
real, nothing tangible – nothing that glowed with the
sort of warmth he had read that childhood memories
should glow with.

How to bring it back – if 'it' existed?

He remembered, vaguely, studying for exams as an

undergraduate – or was it someone else he had read about, studying? He screwed his eyes shut and concentrated – yes, something was back there, somewhere; a past, of sorts, seemed to be taking shape. He could see himself in a run-down student-flat, a flat shared with someone called . . . Jimmy, was it? He remembered thick textbooks and bones – yes, that was it – Jimmy had been studying medicine.

The picture was slowly becoming clearer, his memory tuning in.

John himself had been studying Arts, he recalled, majoring in English and Philosophy.

'I have a theory, John,' Jimmy had once told him, as they sat studying at the kitchen table. 'That the brain is a muscle.'

John had looked up reluctantly from his own books: 'Sorry?'

'Like a muscle it can be strengthened by regular exercise.'

'I don't follow.'

'Built up by skimming through a hundredweight or so of Recommended Reading each day.'

Sitting at the kitchen table, decanting a flagon of red wine into a pair of chipped coffee mugs, Jimmy boasted of his plans to snatch whole chapters of knowledge clean into his head and hold them there effortlessly. He conjured pen and paper from somewhere in his jeans and began to draw up a wine-stained schedule of texts to be studied: a schedule which listed the daily quota of reading not by subject, or page numbers, but by *weight*.

'Easier than counting pages,' he explained, and rose

and taped his list to the door of the fridge.

Gray's Anatomy – 5.4 kilos
Harrison's Internal Medicine – 7.9 kilos
Robbins' Pathology – 5 kilos exactly

Each day he hoped to lift – to memorise – an extra increment. Was it possible, he speculated, to weigh the brain Before and After? Would there be a measurable difference: the actual *weight* of a memory?

'And what of you, John?'

'Me?'

'You. Have you measured the weight of your philosophy texts?'

'I don't really see the need.'

'No? I must prepare you a training schedule for Philosophy. Fetch me the kitchen scales.'

Setting up the scales, he began to weigh the books, jotting down the figures.

Heidegger's Being and Time – 165 grams
Sartre's Being and Nothingness – 95 grams
Parfit's Personal Identity – 62. 5 grams

'Rather light reading, John,' he said, taping the list to the fridge beneath his own. 'The comparison is not flattering.'

There had always been something a little crazy about Jimmy Best (*now* the name came back). There was something hurried, scurrying, overactive; although not so much in his body as in his mind. And in his mouth.

'What about novels?' he asked. 'Perhaps your Eng. Lit. reading list is a little weightier.'

John handed over *The Great Gatsby* – his current assignment – and watched as the needle flickered up to 125 measly grams. *Ulysses* weighed in at a still unimpressive 1.3 kilos. Then he remembered the ten thick volumes of Proust.

But Jimmy was already off on another tangent. From his reading of Pavlov – Medical Psychology 1A – he had developed the idea of the brain as a performing dog, he announced. He didn't subscribe to punishment theory – but always rewarded the dog when it was good.

'Fido has a sweet tooth,' he confided.

'Sorry?'

'Fido,' he explained, tapping his head, 'has a fondness for chocolates, toffees, confectionery.'

Still talking, he began to produce sticky clumps of Mixed Sweets from various denim orifices – itemising aloud his intended study-method with each. He would suck only lime jubes while memorising Anatomy. For Physiology he would chew on chocolate-coated licorice bullets, and for Biochemistry jelly mint-leaves: the pale-green ones, frosted with tiny crystals of sugar.

Surely the resonances evoked by the different tastes would prove useful. Especially in exams. Slip the relevant sweet into his mouth – a butterscotch, say, or marzipan – and everything would come back. He planned to walk into the exam-hall with bulging pockets. Even during orals he intended to be constantly reaching into his pockets.

Or so he told John, acting out all the various roles in his reverie:

'What have you got there, Best?'

'Where?'

'In your pockets.'

'Sustenance, Professor.'

'Highly irregular, Best.'

'I'm a diabetic.'

A small lie, but necessary in the circumstances, he laughingly defended himself.

'Not that anyone could accuse me of *cheating*, of course.'

'Of course.'

'Others use mnemonic aids – nonsense rhymes, acronyms. Who could object to a jelly bean?'

Jimmy seemed to go to enormous lengths for a laugh. Or did he merely improvise, using whatever materials were at hand: mixed sweets, kitchen scales? Whichever, in this mood he was always unstoppable.

'Why not apply the principle to your philosophy studies, John?'

'Well . . .'

'I have just the thing for you,' he announced. 'Albeit on a grander, more calorie-intensive scale.'

He vanished out the door, returning in five minutes with a huge, almost weightless bag of assorted cakes and buns.

'Let's see,' he murmured, carefully setting out his purchases on the table. 'For Logic you must consume only . . . ah, cream puffs. For Epistemology a lamington or two. What else?'

'Ethics?'

'Chocolate eclairs, I think.'

John had other ideas. The novels on the table before him waited to be re-read – he dreaded the task. Perhaps Jimmy's methods could help. He began planning his menu for the week. A fried kidney, swimming in butter. A small cake, dipped in tea.

By the end of the week he had gained a few kilos – at least *some* of which was knowledge, possibly – when his housemate reported that the method was not without its flaws.

'I'm beginning to exhaust the taste-options,' Jimmy announced, deadpan. Another reverie followed. The sheer *quantity* of knowledge had the number of possible sweets outnumbered completely, he improvised. The blander stuff – the barley sugars and licorice allsorts and jelly raspberries – no longer seemed to work. His jaded palate was forced to seek out more aromatic flavours: hot eucalyptus jujubes, musk LifeSavers, volatile spearmints and peppermints, pungent aniseed balls. Sweets that not so much melted in the mouth as fumed.

Remembering all this, back in the present, driving home from the doctor's, John found himself suddenly ravenous.

Certain tastes – a single drop of wine, a crumb of food clinging to the palate – could evoke whole floods of memories, perhaps. But with him the effect worked far better in reverse: the memories conjured forth a flood of saliva.

He walked to the fridge as soon as he arrived home: nothing. He picked up his keys, and headed for the door. Perhaps the Deli would have some pastries: some lamington or vanilla slice that he might slowly chew, and in chewing restore to his mind something else from his childhood: some remembrance of something past that he could cling to, an unarguable *proof* of his identity.

XVII

CHAPTER SEVEN
THE FRECKLE COUNT

His stomach full, John still felt in other respects hugely dissatisfied. Especially with regard to who – or what – he was. Nothing much had surfaced: no 'real' world to pin himself to. Anecdotal student memories were all very well, but too typical – too much a part of every student's past. He needed some sort of touchstone: some objective data, or even measurements, with which he could compare himself later, to see if he was – as he suspected – changing.

Or being changed.

He gazed into the mirror; his freckled Celtic face

stared back. And there he had it! He suddenly remembered counting his freckles once, years ago, during the desperate self-preoccupied terrors of adolescence.

He had not been a pretty sight as a teenager: always sunburnt and peeling, always pimpled and, above all, freckled.

And so he had attempted to measure, to *quantify*, the extent of that disfigurement, late one night. He could still recall the total: 2,454 freckles, give or take a dozen or so hiding above the hair-line, or deep in an orifice.

The task hadn't been easy and took the better part of the night. But why not repeat the count now? He had plenty of time. If he were a fictional character, as he increasingly suspected – nothing more than a cluster of images and scraps of conversation kept aloft by some unreliable, unstable imagination – then the freckle counts would vary, surely.

Not even a Flaubert would remember the exact number of freckles on all his creations from one day to the next.

Armed with a thick felt-tip pen, he stripped off his clothes and entered the bathroom. Standing before the mirror, he divided his body with deft pen-strokes into chunky butcher segments: rumps, shanks, loins, legs, and a selection of other, choicer cuts. He then began counting the freckles in each segment, planning to sum the lot.

He had completed both hind legs and a portion of rump when he heard the key in the door, and Jasmine's image appeared in the mirror. She was standing behind him, staring incredulously.

'Having fun?'

'I'm counting.'

'Counting ?'

'My freckles.'

She eyed him slowly up and down: her husband, standing naked in front of the hall mirror, watching her reflected in the glass, and covered with strange inky patterns.

'Have you been drinking?'

'No.'

'Let me smell your breath.'

He kept his back to her, still half-absorbed in his self-inspection, not wanting to lose count. 'No.'

'Is this some kind of joke?'

'Not at all. It couldn't be more serious.'

She shook her head, worried. 'How many freckles so far?'

'You've made me lose count. I'll have to start again. Look – maybe you could help? We never seem to do things together anymore. There's a small area on my back – the sacrum – I just can't reach.'

'It looks like a big job.'

'A few minutes at most.'

She began backing away: 'Look – I don't want any trouble. I only came to get my things.'

He watched her growing smaller in the mirror. 'It's not what it looks. Nothing kinky. I just wanted to check the number. I have a suspicion that I'm changing. That everything about me is changing, or being changed.'

'You're being *what*?'

'Altered. I thought I could catch them out.'

'Them? Who on earth is *them*?'

'The controllers. God. The Force. The Text. Who-ever.'

'Jesus Christ,' she whispered.

'Him, too,' he said, but before he could explain further she was out the door, slamming it after her, her footsteps running away down the drive, back to the safe haven of her office at Medusa publishing.

XVIII

CHAPTER EIGHT
A SELF-PORTRAIT OF THE ARTIST

John gazed at his reflection in the mirror. No one seemed to believe that he was changing. Not Jasmine. Not even the family GP accepted that there was anything seriously amiss. How to prove it – and above all to himself?

Keeping some sort of record seemed the best idea, some kind of graph, or flow-sheet, of the changes.

Which meant drawing up a personal inventory, a self-portrait. And since oils – or even water-colours – were not his field, he was left with words.

But where to begin? How to go about the task? He

had read his share of novels, could summon up any number of stock components, anatomical bits and pieces that might be fitted together, police-artist fashion, into a self-portrait.

But which to choose? In the kitchen he began to scribble out a list of parts. Aquiline Nose? Roman Brow? Thick Sensuous Lips? Or Lips Thin and Cruel? High Slavic Cheekbones? Low Sloping Forehead? Elfin smile? Or Leprechaun? Weak Chin, or Strong? With or without Cleft?

And the eyes? Hooded? Predatory? Hollow? Sunken? Mad? Staring? Blue? Piercing? Steel-Grey? Warm? Brown? Jade-Green?

Or none of the above? He returned to the bathroom and examined his reflection in the mirror. It occured to him that his features were dominated not by his eyes but his eye*brow*. Singular. He only possessed one: a long, thin bush, growing even thinner in the middle, shared equally by both eyes.

Three inches lower and that eyebrow would have made a fine moustache. His eyes were often drawn to it as he shaved, stuck up there on the forehead. Worn permanently skewed to one side, it was capable of great feats of superciliousness.

What else? The hair – thick, forward-flopping – needed to be continually pushed back. The eyes – no avoiding the verb – twinkled. And his mouth? Big, in a word.

He was – or always had been – a great talker. Did he talk so much because of the size of his mouth? Even when it was closed, words seemed to, well, *leak* out.

Enough, though, of the face. What of height?

Weight? Identifying marks and tattooes? He could recall no scars or birthmarks. And as for the freckles . . .

Actual dimensions were easier to estimate. He was short: five-six, five-seven. And not more than one hundred and thirty pounds in weight, maybe even one hundred and twenty. Which was what in metric? sixty kilos? sixty-five?

And the clothes? As he inspected himself, he realised that one thing, at least, had remained unchanged. He was wearing the same clothes he had been wearing twenty years before, as an undergraduate. Not the actual same clothes, of course – he had changed – but the same *sort* of clothes: the student uniform of cords and leather-elbowed jacket, desert boots. Had he ever worn a suit? He removed the coat and examined the shirt beneath. Even this had remained unchanged: military style, epaulettes, button-down pockets.

He noticed suddenly, on the armpits of the shirt, that rings of dried sweat could be counted, spreading concentrically. The number of days since he had last changed that shirt could be calculated exactly, in the manner of dating tree-trunks . . . one, two, three, four . . . five.

He was letting himself go.

CHAPTER NINE
MORE TABASCO

Friday night. The weekend had begun.

Bennett was standing at the bus-stop alone, when the woman, a stranger, joined him. Night was falling: she emerged from the surrounding darkness without warning, almost as if materialising in the glow of the street-light above.

She took up position slightly in front of him, as if inviting inspection. Her hair was knotted behind in a thick chignon; his eyes were drawn to the way it was parted in the middle by a delicate line that dipped slightly as it followed the incurvation of her skull.

She glanced up and down the dark road and then turned slightly towards him. 'The buses are hopeless at this time of night.'

Her eyes looked strangely large. As she turned, her face moved into the light, and then out: her eyes, momentarily dark blue, darkened again. She was close to him: closer than a stranger might usually stand, yet not quite within what he regarded as his intimate space. He stared into those eyes, fascinated: they had, as it were, layers of successive colours, which were denser at the bottom, and grew lighter towards the surface of the cornea.

'Are you going to the city?' she asked.

He nodded, still intrigued by her appearance. Was she headed for a fancy dress ball? She was wearing a full summer dress with what he somehow knew vaguely to be flounces; a dress that was yellow, wide in the waist, and long in the skirt. As she stood, swaying a little in the gentle breeze, the skirt alternately ballooned and dimpled with the impress of her body.

'I've a suggestion,' she said. 'Why don't we share a cab? For the cost of two bus tickets . . . '

'Fine by me,' he agreed, a little too quickly. 'Unless the bus comes first.'

Already he was hoping that it wouldn't. Seeming to answer his prayer, a cab emerged into the circle of light, as if from the dark wings of a stage, and pulled up opposite. He watched, eagerly, as it disgorged a single passenger, U-turned and pulled up again in front of the bus-stop.

He hadn't seen her hail the cab; perhaps some subtle gesture had been hidden from him.

'What's your name?' he asked as he climbed in after her.

'Emma,' she said, simply, and he was a little surprised she didn't ask his name in return.

'I feel I know you,' he said. 'Something familiar. I can't quite put my finger on it.'

She was wearing perfume – French, he suspected. Her knee beneath the full skirt rested gently against his. He felt his heart turning over, the blood rushing to his head in response to it, and her overwhelming presence.

He had not believed such sudden lust was possible. Mostly his seductions had been matters of patient build-up. A meal, wine, amusing conversation: the slow growth of desire he had always needed to seduce himself as much as the object of his desire. He even suspected at times he was too slow for his women – that they would have preferred something more sudden, more violent.

'Where to?' the cabbie asked.

'The city,' he somehow got out; then, heart hammering, turned to his companion to speak, but she placed a finger on his lips to silence him, and then removed the finger and replaced it with her own soft lips.

At this, the cab, a lumbering Valiant, set out. It drove some miles up South Road, crossed the Emerson overpass, turned right into Anzac Highway, and crossed the Keswick Bridge.

'Go on,' came a voice from the backseat; perhaps *his* voice.

The cab set off again, and soon it came to Victoria

Square, and the line of cab-ranks outside the Hilton.

'No, straight on,' came the same voice.

The cab moved back into the night traffic, travelling north through the Pirie street intersection, and made its third halt at the top of Rundle Mall.

'Keep going, will you,' came the voice, furiously.

And at once resuming its course, it passed by the Festival Centre, and the Cathedral, drove up into North Adelaide, detoured randomly along Rose Street, Prospect, then travelled the entire length of Main North Road to Gepps Cross.

From there it returned, and then, without any fixed plan or direction, wandered about at random. The battered taxi was seen outside the university in North Terrace and alongside Flash Gelateria in Hindley Street; also, briefly, on Windy Point and the summit of Mount Lofty. It drove the entire length of the South Eastern Freeway, then further south to Tailem Bend, and back across the Wellington ferry to Strathalbyn, and along the lonely crest of Hack Range Road, Echunga.

From time to time the cabbie cast despairing eyes at passing pubs, filled with Friday night drinkers – he had missed tea. But he fully understood the furious desire for locomotion that urged this couple in the backseat never to stop.

How could he *not* understand what was happening in the backseat? It would be the most ludicrous fiction to suggest that such naivety was possible.

Once or twice he asked if it would be much longer, and at once exclamations of anger burst forth from behind him, and he drove on, tilting his mirror vainly for a better view of the dark recesses of the backseat behind him, watching in the end quite contentedly as the meter ticked over.

In Kangarilla, the Salvation Army band opened large wonder-stricken eyes as the cab circled the main square a good fifteen times, slowly, rocking mysteriously, and then suddenly took off, roaring, along the dark Adelaide road.

At about four on the Saturday morning, the taxi stopped in a back street in Glenelg, and a woman got out and walked away without turning her head.

'That'll be three hundred and twenty-two dollars,' the cabbie said as Bennett straightened his tie. 'Plus tip.'

CHAPTER TEN
SUBJECT, OBJECT, AND THE NATURE OF REALITY

As the taxi carrying Bennett and his mysterious companion drove off into the night, darkness also enveloped the distant house which, only that Friday morning, Bennett had left shining in the sun.

Squatting upon its now black, secluded acres, with lights all out and the moon sunk, the house suffered a downpouring of immense darkness. Nothing it seemed could survive the flood, the profusion of darkness that crept in at keyholes and crevices, stole round window-blinds, infiltrated bedrooms, swallowed up here an empty wine bottle and an unwashed, crusted glass, there the forgotten and unrefrigerated remains of a roast asquirm with diligent little operatives; and there again the sprung seams of an imploding tea-chest ballasted with *Weekend Australians*, doubling as occasional table. Not only was the furniture confounded (for, in the shifting glooms, the kitchen table seemed no longer there, or was at least evanescent, waxing and waning in dark ebbs and flows of objective reality), but there was scarcely anything left of body or mind by which one could say, 'This is Bennett', (or indeed, 'John'), or 'This is Jasmine.'

Nothing stirred in the lounge room or in the kitchen; and if there had been a staircase, nothing would have stirred on it either. Only through slack hinges and heat-stretched woodwork certain airs detached from the body of the wind as certain airs detach themselves from the human body (house and body being respectively ramshackle and pampered after all), crept round corners and ventured indoors. Almost one might imagine them as they entered the various rooms, questioning and wondering, tugging at handles to find the intimacies of drawers, puffing eagerly into bedrooms in hopes of surprising a lustily bouncing mattress. (Here, Bennett in the bouncing back of the taxi, blew out his candle. It was past midnight). Dirty little airs! whisper the fingered and probed and stroked walls and wallpapers and air-tickled French letters abandoned in the wastepaper basket and the three-week old Dead Roses (of which the stalks, sprigged with thorn, might, had they been given voice, have proclaimed the paradox of man in Christ and Christ in man, knowing rock for what it was, or might have been, and stone as the substance of bare conflict. Which might have done, in the end. When there were only the trees. And of course the roses. Which, in the immense silence.

Stood breathing. Though dead.)

Were they allies? Were they enemies? asked the little airs of each lewdly molested artefact and item of the penetralia. At length, all sighed together, desisting; all together gave off an aimless gust, a circumstance not unknown between those walls and under that roof – during Bennett's incumbency at least, for who can speak for John? Though, in contrast to the night silence that greeted *this* aimless gust, Bennett was given to saluting such audible moments of nether exhalation with a shouted 'Hooray' or the curious query, 'Another bun, Vicar?' accompanied by a creaking lifting of the leg.

But what, after all, is one night? It is . . . one night. It is the space between the end of the previous day, *qua* day, and the beginning of the ensuing. It is two effulgences straddling the absence of effulgence, *qua* effulgence. It is from the going down of the sun thereof to the emergence of Phoebus's car from its russett carport for reasons unknown but time will tell. Only once in that night, a sheet of galvanised iron partly detached itself from the body of the house and clanked for a moment mournfully; and possibly once, on the notional landing a putative board theoretically sprang; and once in the middle of the night with a roar a tree fell demolishing three rooms at the southern end. Then, again, peace – like the tree – descended, apart from a distant warbling that might have been the outrage of an unroofed magpie. Had there been a light-house nearby, its wavering beam, like a footfall, would have passed in adoring obeisance to its own image across walls and mirrors and smashed framework and crumpled roof: but there was not, so it did not. Some time during the hours that followed, the leaves of the calendar flipped over twice, bringing at last on a bright and blowy Monday morning, Mrs Van Ness to tear the veil of silence (and also her dress – on a nail newly naked after the nights' destructions). Clattering through the front door in the loud, sensible shoes that had hacked youthful ankles while relentlessly queue-jumping in refectory or registry and gesturing impa-tiently with those hands that had penned awesome mature-age essays, Mrs Van Ness set about flicking a contemptuous duster over the more accessible bits of Bennett's disintegrating menage.

CHAPTER ELEVEN
MONDAY MORNING

John stood outside Amanda Carrington's house. His watch told him that it was early morning – the smallest hours of Monday morning – and that therefore two whole days must have elapsed. He had vague recollections of waiting at the bus-stop – surely that had been on Friday evening, the start of the weekend? – and of meeting someone there; but at that point his memory seemed deliberately to shut down, refusing to allow him further access.

Waves of panic churned his stomach and made his head spin. Where had he been? What had he done?

Was the State Transport Authority as slow as that? Two days from Bedford Park to the City? Possible, but improbable.

At length he squared his shoulders, stepped through Amanda Carrington's gateway and, amid scents of lavender bush and overhanging rose, pushed on the doorbell. In the depths a muffled electronic dong-dong could be heard, a dying fall. He pressed three times more and rapped on the leadlight windowpane flanking the door before a light glimmered somewhere inside and, after much chain rattling, the door opened.

Amanda was wrapped in a thin gown with some sort of Batik design apppearing and disappearing according to its – and her – folds.

She looked bemused and said, *For God's sake* twice before adding, *You look terrible.*

'I'm sorry to arrive on your step unnanounced like this, Amanda, but I . . . '

'It's all right. Come in. Are you ill? Would you like some coffee?'

'No. Look I . . . I need to . . . '

'John, darling, what on earth is the matter?'

John winced at the name, a reminder of his plight, but plunged on.

'Amanda, I've forgotten – I've forgotten . . . '

'Your car keys?'

'No, no, it's . . . '

'Your condoms?'

He looked up sharply to see if she was teasing him, but she seemed entirely serious.

'. . . worse than that. I've forgotten . . . '

'Your way home!'

'. . . everything: my past, my childhood, my name, *every*thing.'

'My God. That *is* careless.'

'My name. Even my *name*,' he said hopelessly.

'You've had . . . what do they call it? Some sort of fugue. Amnesia. You might have bumped your head. Do you remember falling . . . Come in, sit down and collect yourself a bit. We'll sort it all out.'

They sat facing each other in the soft glow of a single lamp. Between them, on a small table, Amanda soon set down a coffee pot, milk in a jug, and a plate of chocolate biscuits. She had more or less planted him bodily on the sofa where he sat passive and stunned while she made coffee.

'Now!' she said. 'Without especially trying, just nice and easy, tell me something from your childhood. Any childhood memory.'

'Looking back on it,' John began in a halting low voice, ' it's like a mess of memories and impressions scattered and clotted and pasted together like a mulch of fallen leaves on a damp autumn pavement. Naturally, the first memory is of a childhood shared: my brother Jack and me. He was only three years my senior but . . . '

The words had suddenly come more easily; Amanda sat forward, her brow furrowing. She interrupted him abruptly.

'Okay. Good. Fast forward it a bit now, to some other memory. Or rewind if you like. But find a different episode or sequence.'

'A very good time it was,' John said immediately. 'A good time for Baby Tuckoo. Sometimes the bed would be wet and be all warm and later cold . . .'

'Fine. That's fine. Try again. Put it . . . put it in, ah, *different* words.'

'I was born in the year 1894 . . . My father left just after this, taking with him my two older brothers. The world could not be flat because of the hills – we children settled that among ourselves. Later on we decided it couldn't be round, for the same reason. But we took it for granted, what we saw of it. The sky was part of the world, of course, and a dome, just as we saw it, and it ended all round where it touched the hills or flats. *Nous etions à l'étude, quand le Proviseur entra, suivi d'un* nouveau *habillé en bourgeois et d'un garçon de classe qui portait un grand pupitre. Ceux qui dormaient se reveillèrent, et chacun se leva comme surpris dans son travail.*'

'All right, John. All right. You know I don't speak French. Perhaps if you . . .'

John nodded vaguely, seeming anxious to continue.

'I do not wish to name the village where all this took place,' he continued in the same monotone. 'Suffice to say, I became one of those who always have a lance in the rack, an ancient shield, a lean hack and a grey-hound for coursing. My habitual diet consisted of a stew, more beef than mutton, of hash most nights, boiled bones on Saturdays, lentils on Fridays, and a young pigeon as a Sunday treat; and on this I spent three quarters of my income. Of course, all happy families are alike but an unhappy family is unhappy after its own fashion. When everything went wrong in our household, on a very hot evening at the beginning of July, I left my little room at the top of a house in

Carpenter Lane, went out into the street, and, unable to make up my mind, walked slowly in the direction of Kokushkin Bridge. For whenever I find myself growing grim about the mouth; whenever it is a damp drizzly November in my soul; whenever I find myself involuntarily pausing before coffin warehouses and bringing up the rear of every funeral I meet; and especially whenever my hypos get such an upper hand of me that it requires a strong moral principle to prevent me from deliberately stepping into the street, and methodically knocking people's hats off, then I account it high time to get to sea as soon as I can. Given the existence as uttered forth in the public works of Puncher and Wattmann of a personal God *quaquaquaqua* with white beard *quaquaquaqua* outside time without extension who from the heights of divine apathia divine aphasia loves us dearly with some exceptions for reasons unknown but time . . . '

John, whose eyes had glazed during this monologue, seemed to recover himself, and faltered into silence. He felt confused, embarrassed. Amanda was roaming the bookcases that covered two of the room's walls. She returned to her armchair and tumbled several books onto the table between them. He glimpsed among them Tolstoy, Flaubert, Melville, Cervantes.

'These are only the ones I recognised,' she said. 'What you've just told me is a hotch-potch of literary childhoods and beginnings. None of that was about *you*.'

John's tense, set features seemed to collapse.

'That's the point,' he said. 'I can't *remember* my own past. Or at least, that's what I thought to begin with,

97

when all this started. But I'm gradually arriving at a different conclusion.'

'What do you mean?'

A peculiar, expectant smile momentarily lit up John's mournful face.

'Okay, Amanda. Your turn. You're feeling concerned for me – but let's see how *you* handle this test. Tell me about *your* childhood.'

'That's ridiculous. What do you mean? I was . . . was . . . I remember that I . . . '

She looked at him, stricken, then seemed about to resume.

'Don't worry,' John said wearily. 'You'll dredge something up, no doubt, but it'll be automatic, regurgitated stuff, like my "past".'

'What does all this mean? What are you telling me?'

The blood had drained from her face; she seemed as pale as a mannequin in a window display.

'Think it through,' John said. 'First, I have no surname and seemingly have never had one. You don't know it, I don't know it. Second, my past is a mere hotchpotch. When I try to recall and recount it, I come out with a lot of ready-made rubbish, as if . . . as if I might get too close to some truth about myself . . . about us, if I was allowed to ponder it and think it through. As if my controllers, my . . . authors, so to speak, get a bit anxious if I get too close to . . . '

Once again he broke off, looking excited yet also confused. Then, with a visible effort: 'I'll come back to that in a minute. Now. Third, tell me this. Who is Jasmine?'

'Jasmine?'

'Jasmine.'

'John, she's your wife. You live with her.'

'But *you've* never seen her,' John pounced. 'You ask after her, I tell you about her. But you've never seen her. And, as a matter of fact, neither have I – except once, fleetingly, in a mirror.'

'What! What on earth . . . '

'She's in my head. She has certain traits – like resounding bouts of pre-menstrual tension and long shapely legs and a throaty moan at certain moments. And she works for Medusa publishing. But she's not actually *around*. It's as if these traits have been grafted into my mental world. But she's not actual. And listen to this. Fourth . . . '

John stood up and began pacing the room, as if unable to contain a towering sense of impatience.

'Fourth, think about Professor Harp and the Flanders Fields University of the South Pacific and the ASIO Chair and the RSL Chair and the Signals Corps Chair, and so on. Can you imagine that sort of thing actually happening in the real world? Can you imagine a narrow-minded, vindictive, literature-hating little shit like Harp actually being a university Professor of English? Well – maybe *that*. But surely not the army sponsoring chairs? Or a university at Woomera? The Nippon Retirement Centre? That's mad stuff, all that. Parody – and bad parody at that. It wouldn't happen in the real world. Just the same as people don't forget their entire childhood and they don't find themselves confused about their name . . . '

'Supposing all you say has some point, what is it? What are you driving at?'

Amanda was calmer now, challenging, more like her old self.

'This is the point,' John said, turning round to face her as if about to address a jury. ' This is the point: we are in some sort of story. We are made-up characters – *fictional* characters. We are flat, two-dimensional. We aren't *convincing* – we can't even convince ourselves. We have no will, no history, no control over our actions or our roles. Only last Friday morning I . . . Oh, never mind. Just believe me. We are *fictions* !'

'No! You've flipped, John. You've cracked.'

'We are the creatures of an imagination somewhere. Or . . . this is what I was trying to say before . . . perhaps two or more separate and *different* imaginations. Because there's another dimension to all this that I can't understand or get hold of. My personality seems to be *split*.'

'Schizoid,' she murmured, knowingly. 'You *have* cracked.'

'Where was I for the past two days? Why do I remember, though I involuntarily try to repress, a taxi ride . . . I was taken for a ride, in every sense. Though my name wasn't John. Or did I have . . . '

Uncertainty overwhelmed him, showed in his face and suddenly irresolute movements. Amanda looked at him.

'You need help,' she said. ' You need help, John.'

'So you don't believe me? You don't accept that all the evidence, none of which you've refuted incidentally, points to our being . . . made up?'

'No, I don't,' she said in a muted voice and with a kind of forced conviction.

'Well, I do,' John said. 'I *know* that I am a fiction, a *circus animal*,' he added with a note of triumph as if at last he had hit upon the right words. 'And so are you and so is everything connected with us, caught up in the same dream.'

'But if that's so, what happens when we *know*? What happens when the circus animals desert?'

The room had been growing slowly darker: at first John put this down to the oncoming night; but things around him were losing definition: the books on the coffee table becoming blurred, Amanda herself becoming misty around the edges. He rubbed at his eyes, and when he reopened them the room and everything else within it and outside of it had disappeared. Overhead, one by one, the stars were going out.

John floated alone in a huge, illimitable grey and silent void. No life was visible. No features of any kind disturbed the even monotony of grey.

It gave him no pleasure at all to realise that he had been absolutely right.

LIMBO

Either the enveloping fog was cold, or he was dank with fear.

More likely the latter, he assumed, because the grey swirl had a quality of nothingness, an impression of absence: not the clammy tendrilling of fog but an uncanny neutrality.

He groped his way forward – or was it to one side? Or even backwards? Or was he actually moving at all? There was nothing by which to measure progress or movement. Only when he knew he was at the edge of panic – in the same moment claustrophobic yet paradoxically immobilised by a sense of limitless space about him – was he saved by a glimpse of *something*: the barest faltering, so to speak, in the circumambient vacuity.

It was a building. A sort of dome. A large sign outside proclaimed:

MALLEY AND DAUGHTERS
LITERARY CHARACTER AGENCY

ROLE AUDITIONS, COACHING, CONTRACT ADVICE
COMPREHENSIVE CASTING SERVICE
FRANCHISES HELD FOR A LARGE RANGE OF FICTIONS

He grasped in an instant the purpose of the place, and headed for the entrance. Double glass doors sighed inwards as he approached and murmured shut behind him . . .

– Malley and Daughters? he asked doubtfully of the trim young woman who emerged from a nearby office to greet him.

– Una Malley, she smiled. One of the daughters. Can I help?

– I've come hoping to find some sort of employment. As a . . . as a character in the works of various of your authors.

He spoke the words as if he could scarcely believe what he was asking; which indeed he scarcely could.

– Of course! Come on in. Coffee?

– I prefer tea.

He followed her into a narrow, book-lined study.

'You are looking for something in particular? Cameo roles?'

He jumped, a little startled by the change in her voice. She was still speaking English, the voice was still *hers*, but the tone had changed, subtly. There was a feeling of her words being somehow more objective, less urgent, set back, as if in quotation marks, for closer study.

'Something different.' he said. '*Anything* different.'

'Different? Then you have *some* experience in this line of work.'

'More than I need.'

'Do you mind if I take some notes? No? Fine. Um . . . What line of fiction have you been working in before?'

'Academic spoofs, mostly. Comic university novels.'

'David Lodge kind of thing?'

'Yes. I suppose. Only much better written.'

'Isn't *every*thing? Milk? Sugar? But I can understand your desire for a change. There's so much of it around.'

'It's not that. I enjoy university life. I've been well looked after, fictionally. Until recently. It's all come as a bit of a shock. Lately I seem to be caught up in some sort of . . . well, *battle* between different authors. I feel I'm being torn apart. Like a kid in a custody dispute. I'm looking for a way out. Something completely different.'

'Would you like to travel? Something out of the country?'

'That would be wonderful. Some kind of working holiday perhaps?'

'Let's see . . . we have something coming up in

104

Europe. A small part in Czechoslovakia. I'll be frank –
the role is difficult. People seem to find the part something of a trial. It has a high turnover.'

'As I said, I'm ready for anything. I've never been
there, but I've heard that Prague is a beautiful city.
Will I need to take anything? Passport? Visa?
Toothbrush.'

'Uh, I doubt if you'll be needing a toothbrush.'

She seemed embarrassed as she said this, avoiding
his gaze, and rushed on before he could press her for
details. 'We'll handle that side. And your accomoda-
tion. Something near the Fürstenberg Garden. With a
view of the castle. All *you* have to do is close your eyes.
And please . . .'

'Yes?'

'Don't call us, we'll call you.'

As he awoke the next morning from uneasy dreams,
he found himself transformed into a gigantic letter K.

He was lying on the hard back-spine of the letter,
and when he lifted and waggled his two angular legs
the bed quilt could hardly keep in position and
seemed about to slip off completely.

Mein Gott, he thought. What has happened? And
why am I thinking in German? Who am I? K.? K.
what?

He found he couldn't even remember the other letters in his name. His eyes turned to the window of his
room, through which, high on the hill in the distance,
he could see, as promised, the castle. He felt drawn
towards the walls, as if some sort of answer, or anti-

dote, to his predicament lay beyond. Wiggling his legs frantically, he struggled out of bed, falling to the floor with a distinct clatter, as if he were made of china, or some kind of hard plastic. The exertion, however, tired him enormously, and he became aware that while he had a ramrod spine, and two legs set at forty-five degree angles to it, with a right angle between *them*, he was unequipped with lungs; and was finding it increasingly difficult to breath.

Nor could he call for help: he had no mouth, no tongue – no *teeth*.

He twisted his rigid backbone violently, but eventually sank back to the floor, and from his nostrils, wherever they were, emerged the last faint flicker of breath.

When the cleaner arrived early in the morning, she took her customary peep into his room. Since she happened to have a long-handled broom in her hand she tried to tickle K. with it from the doorway. She poked harder, and only when she had pushed the dead letter some distance along the floor without meeting any resistance was her attention fully aroused, and she swept it from the house completely.

No sooner had she turned her back than a magpie – mistaking K. for a large pretzel, or small edible snake, frozen in some stiff, angular configuration by rigor-mortis – removed him, or it, with one deft swoop from the doorstep.

He opened his eyes, blinking.

'Back already?' Una Malley's voice said.

'Things didn't work out.'

'Disappointed in Prague?'

'I didn't see much of Prague. I guess I was looking for a kind of working holiday. The problem was the work. Who was in charge? And what is he, some kind of sadist?'

'He's very highly respected in his field.'

'He should work in a penal settlement. Dreaming up tortures!'

'I believe he has some work in that line available. I could check if you wish.'

'No *thank* you. Something a little less exotic.'

'America? Okay? Close your eyes.'

'When in doubt, bring in a man with a gun,' he thought he heard someone, or something, murmur somewhere. And there he was, himself, gun in hand, moving through a door.

For a big man, he moved surprisingly fast.

Doll-face was tied to the bed, one limb roped to each corner. Her body looked like it was poured out of honey. Little weasel-face was standing over her, a small man with a big gun.

'Drop the hardware, weasel-face,' he said, 'Then untie the floozie.'

For a little man he moved surprisingly slow.

'You won't get away with this,' weasel-face growled. 'This is consenting adults in private.'

He stepped forward and hit weasel-face right where it doesn't hurt: in the solar plexus. Wind rushed from the weasel-mouth; the weasel-body seemed to implode, as if depressurised – it went down like the Hindenburg.

Stepping over the remains, he untied her.

'Move your sweet butt, doll-face,' he said. 'We're outa here.'

He moved through the doorway, then turned – she hadn't followed.

'Don't call me doll-face,' she told him, pouting. 'I'm not your doll.'

'Okay, babe. Anything you say. Let's just get outa here.'

He could hear heavy footsteps approaching in the passage outside; he hoped it wasn't the Greek.

'Listen, sweetheart. We've got to *move*!'

'No, you listen. I was *working*, you fucker. I was turning a trick – a little goldmine. You just killed my best client!'

'But, babe.'

'I'm not a babe, either. If you want to talk demeaning to me you can *pay* for it.'

He paused, thinking. 'How much?'

She lay back on the bed again. 'Depends on what you want to call me.'

He rolled the notion around inside his head; it came up aces. He hadn't been allowed to use the old role-words, the old gender-words, for years. Christ, it had been against the law for . . . how long?

'Honey?' he suggested. 'Sweet-lips? Baby-doll?'

She shook her head. 'Out of your league. You can't afford them.'

'Luv?' he tried. 'Dear?'

She seemed to be relenting: 'How much of the folding stuff you got?'

He emptied his pockets: a dime, a nickel, and two quarters, whatever they all were.

'None of the folding stuff,' he said. 'Only the hard, round, jingling stuff.'

She gathered up the coins and counted them.

'You can call me Miss,' she said. 'Twice. Cheapskate. Then get the hell out of here.'

He opened his eyes.

'No luck again?'

'I guess I'm not as adventurous as I thought.'

'Perhaps we could find something local. Something quiet, domestic. Do you like Melbourne? Carlton? Are you any good at cleaning hardened grease-dribbles?'

He shook his head.

'No? Something more outdoors? You want to make the first north-south crossing of Australia?'

'Sounds boring. I'm not sure if . . . '

'On camel-back? Singing opera? Having a trans-cendental love affair?'

'What does that mean?'

'It means you don't actually fuck.'

'Forget it.'

'What about sailing up a river on a raft with a glass church?'

'Get real. No one would ever write anything so crazy.'

'Do you fancy something in the wheat fields? Miles and miles of them – and every woman you meet a lesbian?'

They stared at each other in silence for some time: an impasse.

Finally Una shook her head in sympathy.

– You're right. I wouldn't take any of these parts either. But times are tough. We've got the fiction we had to have. Most of the good jobs in this country at present are for women. Still, you are *very* hard to please. There are characters in the camp who would trade everything they have for opportunities like these – including their gender.

Her voice suddenly lost its pleasant, distant, 'quoted' feel – a more urgent tone had returned. And the meaning of her words had an alarming drift. Camp?

– Where? he said. *What* camp?

She eyed him sternly.

– Best to cross that bridge when you come to it, she said.

– Just one more chance, he pleaded. Australian, fine. But what about something non-contemporary? Couldn't I just sneak quietly into some early narrative?

Ms Malley's attractive face seemed to waver, and lose definition.

Employed at last! Scientifically, such a contingency can never have befallen of itself. Yet possessed as I am with the more sterling qualities of a chronicler – these being voracious limpidity, lambent veracity, latent vulgarity, vagrant loquacity, and no trousers. Or, to put it in more allergic form, I account myself the homely bailee of that already-glanced-at license to a talent which, reading men like idiot boards and women like braille, I purposed, anyway as I say, or may not yet have adumbrated, to take certain entries from my diary and undertake certain annotative excursions in order to give the extremely attentive reader a tortured picture of that age-old question – Life!

Twenty-two consecutive issues of the Morphettville Race Book lie on the table before me. Lesser men might quail before this endeavour; and so do I. And let me, dear reader, reveal to you (and to my trusty pipe – auditor of all my philosophies) why I quail. Because I know that all my intuitions are being manipulated by the vile Furphy. He makes me narrator of a story but tells me only half the story. What is the result? I am scapegoat and fool to every tawny tigress in the Riverina, stranded inanely in the Beaudesart, unfrocked and unhorsed. But, you see, I know . . . yes, I know that Nosey Alf is a hermaphrodite; and that Mary O'Halloran disappeared from the plot because she got a part with the Royal Shakespeare Company. I know all this to be true or my name's not . . . not . . . whatever it is.

But such is life my fellow-characters. We're all poor players bluffing and feinting our hour across this or that fiction, only to cheapen down to plotless nonentity. But don't give me any jokes about this being a story told by vulgarians, full of bang and wanky, signifying . . . But there's the rub: those signifiers are the problematical . . .

He found himself staring again at Ms Malley across her still impeccable desk.

– Another blank? she said, as if expecting nothing else.

– Out of the frying pan into the fire, he said. Another character fighting his author, or the other way round.

– A bit too . . .

– Tortuous? Yes. That as well. Perhaps the twentieth century *is* my beat, after all.

But Ms Malley was no longer listening. She had the phone off the hook and was dialling a number.

– I'm afraid it's not as easy as that. After three failures to assign and with no further prospect readily available, I have no choice but to transport you to the camp.

The 'camp'! That sinister word again. He slumped unresisting in his chair. The camp, the swirling nothingness outside, the toils of some impossible fiction . . . what did it matter!

– Okay, he said. Lead on. What could be worse than this?

XXIII

A REVISED COURT RULING

FAMILY COURT OF AUSTRALIA
BARRETT *vs* O'HARE

The court has before it recent submissions from the State, containing fresh evidence of the difficulties that the two parties in the dispute Barrett vs O'Hare (viz. Professor Barrett and Typesetter O'Hare) are having complying with the stipulations laid down in the previous interim judgment of this court.

Taking all matters before it into account the court feels it has no choice but to declare null and void its previous ruling in this matter and pronounce that custody of the fictional character known as 'John', or alternatively, 'Bennett', should be awarded to the State for the sake of his, or its, own welfare.

The court notes that the character has proved uncontrollable and unstable in temperament and behaviour under the terms of the previous judgment. Public acts of copulation in taxi cabs and bizarre sexual practices involving felt-tip pens and mirrors suggest that the moral supervision of this character has been minimal.

Furthermore, subsequent attempted placement of the character within a wide-range of fictional foster-homes both within Australia and abroad (viz. Prague, Los Angeles, the Riverina) proved in each case a disastrous failure, in a totally unsuitable environment.

The court therefore rules that the character, or characters, known as John and/or Bennett be delivered to the Camp for Orphaned Characters for his and/or their own safety and well-being, and to remain therein, until further notice, at the Court's pleasure. Neither author is to be permitted any access to, or contact with, the character for the duration of this ruling.

Dated in Adelaide this 20th day of July, 1992.

A DAY IN THE LIFE OF JOHN

John discerned through the gloom and obscurity a pair of high, pretentious-looking gates. As he strained harder to see ahead, he realised that what he had at first taken to be some sort of long, low continuous structure was in fact a cluster of buildings squatting inside a lofty, many-stranded barbed-wire fence. At each corner and at regular intervals along its four sides, watch-towers were propped on wooden scaffolding. As he drew closer, John could make out hunched, dark-clad figures patrolling the inside of the perimeter; and there were two guards in each tower sitting alongside the unmistakeable outline of a machine-gun.

The sense of almost absurd familiarity that this sight aroused in him now crystallised and John realised he was looking at a concentration camp. But one so perfect, so utterly and slavishly attentive to movie-set detail that it parodied itself. It resembled a model camp, a camera trick on a table top; unblemished, ungrained.

He approached the entrance, at either side of which stood a guard in a lumpy greatcoat. Each wore a helmet and stood in the at-ease position with rifle thrust directly out to the length of the right arm.

'Papers,' barked one of them.

Making a reflex grab at his pockets as a result of this peremptory command, John was staggered to find that he actually *had* some papers: a glimpse of the heading as he handed the sheets over showed them to be some sort of Family Court document.

'Second one today with this sort of stuff,' muttered one of the guards, shuffling the pages suspiciously.

Together they peered at the papers while John stood by, uncomprehending.

'What am I doing here?' he asked eventually.

'What?'

'Why am I here?'

'Well, you've . . . you've been . . . scratched. Like all the rest of 'em.'

'*Scratched?*'

'Revised. Erased. Dropped. Dumped. Edited out of a story for some reason or other. Or changed so much that a new character takes over. These papers seem in order. In you go.'

'You expect me to walk into a concentration camp,' John said.

'Suit yourself,' shrugged the taller guard. 'Stay out here if you want. Nothing to eat, of course. Nothing to do.'

He waved an indifferent arm at the swirling amorphous grey that enveloped them and which, as John knew from his recent wanderings, was apparently endless.

'Okay,' he said, affecting a casualness he did not feel. 'Open up!'

He was scarcely inside the gates before he was greeted by a curiously featureless young man with a vaguely cockney accent

'Top of the morning to you, guv.'

'Hello.'

John felt unaccountably wary.

'Been scratched have we, guv?'

'Well, not quite. Yes and no. It's a bit complicated.

'Mum's the word, guv. My lips are sealed. Of course, most of us here reveal all in due course. There's not much else to talk about really. And we're all in the same boat, so . . . '

'Who are you?'

'Who *was* I, guv. Who was I. Not to put too fine a point on it.'

'Okay. Who were you?'

'A classic, guv. Or very nearly. One of the all-time greats. Jim Copperfield, if you please, sir.'

'You mean *David*?' John asked, shaking the proffered hand.

'*Jim*. Retrenched on page 153 in the first draft. David

got the part – now *there's* a very different kettle of fish. A bit of a goody two-shoes, if you ask me. But then I'm not the author. I was dumped because I had too much to say, and the book would have been twice as long.'

'Rotten luck,' John said. 'To be so close.'

'Worse things happen, young master,' Jim said. 'There's always them that's worse off. Over there – the pale, angry lookin' cove. See him? That's our Heathfield. Heathcliff took over in chapter 3 – probably because "cliff" sounds more dramatic than "field".'

John was beginning to feel slightly giddy.

'What *is* this place?' he asked.

'Well, it's a . . . let's see, how do we usually put it for newcomers. It's a kind of orphanage, I suppose. A camp for orphan characters. The orphans of fiction.'

John, remembering the Family Court 'papers' he had miraculously produced from his pocket, felt a flicker of assurance amid the panic. Perhaps there was some logic in all this . . . His gaze returned to the morose figure of Heathfield, who was standing at a high cyclone-wire fence, his fingers threaded through its interlacements as if he were about to shake it down, gazing with forlorn longing into the adjoining compound.

'That's the women's section,' said Jim, noting the direction of his gaze and anticipating his question. 'Heathfield spends all day at the fence calling out to Aggie Linton.'

'You mean Cathy Li–'

'No. Aggie. Cathy was . . .'

'I think I can guess,' John interrupted, growing tired of these exchanges.

'Come on,' Jim said, taking him by the arm. 'You've a lot of new friends to meet. Over there – the pimply kid is Patrick Daedelus. Ignore him, a real pain in the posterior. Next to him, that cloudy figure – the Visible Man. The author couldn't quite work out how to make him plausibly invisible on the first draft. The little fellow dressed in rags, Barry Twist . . . '

The names largely went in one ear and out the other – half familiar, but never quite gelling. At length John found himself approaching another wire gate. Two men, one of whom immediately struck John as peculiarly, hauntingly familiar, were waiting there, gazing through the wire into the next compound.

'Who's that?' he asked.

'Another novice,' Jim said. 'One of your crew, guv. Just arrived. Didn't catch his name. The dapper cove in the silk suit showing him around – that's Bruce Gatsby.'

John overheard Gatsby speaking to his charge as the wire gate swung open.

'And so we press on, Bennett,' said Gastby. 'Ships against the tide. Let me show you your compound.'

Bennett? The name seemed as familiar to John as the figure. For some reason he was convinced that the name 'Bennett' was important to him; but the moment passed, Copperfield was tugging at his sleeve, tugging him towards another wire gate, and a row of dingy dormitory blocks.

'This is *your* place,' Copperfield said. 'The compound for characters from university novels.'

He held out his hand.

'I can't go in, young master,' he said. 'So I'll wish you luck and see you perhaps another time.'

They shook hands and John, with a deep sigh, walked through the wire gate.

A DAY IN THE LIFE OF BENNETT

Having farewelled Bruce Gatsby, Bennett entered the smaller compound, gazing around, trying to take it all in.

'23768A – eyes fixed on the ground,' came an order barked, amplified, from the nearest tower.

He thought he recognised the faces that stared down from the tower: familiar features from the dust jackets of various of the newer textbooks on Critical Theory.

'Better do what they say,' a not unfriendly voice muttered behind him, and he fell in with a line of prisoners, circling Indian-file within the confines of the yard.

'You must be new here,' the same voice murmured as a whistle blew from the tower, and the circle disintegrated into various smaller arcs, then clumps, of prisoners, who sat or sprawled in the corners of the yard.

He seemed to be an old man, grey-haired, wearing faded corduroys: but his face could have been any age. It seemed strangely bland and featureless, as if sanded or rubbed smooth, like a beach pebble. He had no nose to speak of, and the lips and chin were vestigial.

'I don't understand,' Bennett said. 'Is this some kind of leper colony?'

'If only it were,' the man murmured.

'I feel I know you from somewhere . . . ' Bennett began.

His new friend shrugged. 'I doubt it,' he said. 'I've been here for many years – for as long as I can remember.'

'You've never been out?'

'Out to where.'

The amorphous mouth managed a small, bitter laugh before continuing.

'You know I even reached a second draft.' He allowed himself a self-mocking smile at this small touch of vanity. 'In the third draft I was replaced by a younger man.'

Bennett looked at the other prisoners, or inmates, in their huddled groups. Many of them looked strangely familiar, especially the sizeable contingent that was dressed, like him, in the standard-issue academic uniform of the time: corduroys, jacket and leather elbows. The faces were uniformly disfigured, as if their most prominent features had dropped off, or been covered and compressed by tight stockings, like armed criminals.

'Are all these people here for the same reason?'

His new friend smiled tolerantly.

'We are the abandoned ones,' he said. 'Those whose characters were insufficiently realised. Those endowed with no presence. No real features.'

'There are no women,' Bennett suddenly noticed. 'Where are the women?'

His new friend jerked his thumb in the direction of the huts.

'Women's Camp,' he said. 'That way, which reminds me, perhaps I should show you around.'

'I'd like that.'

'By the way,' he said, and extended his hand, 'James is the name. Lucky James.'

James led him between the huts, through another excercise yard filled with a differently clothed breed of inmates – clad in greasy overalls, or covered in coal-grime and wearing miner's helmets – although the faces beneath the helmets and cloth caps remained as difficult to characterise as those in what he was already beginning to think of as 'his' camp. Without exception they were wearing red triangles sewn to their clothing; which made Bennett remember that all the inmates in *his* camp had been wearing small brown-corduroy triangles.

'Social Realism Compound. Crammed with Noble Proletarians, a largely discontinued line of characters these days,' James explained, and led him through the thick crowd of workers and up to a single thickness wire-fence.

'The Women's Camp,' he announced.

And Bennett was suddenly gazing into a vision of heaven. He had never before seen such women, outside of the glossy centrefolds of Men's magazines, or perhaps in the finalists' parade in some beauty pageant he had surreptitiously watched on television. Golden bodies, loose abandoned heads of hair and pouting mouths framed eyes that seemed to want nothing more than to meet his and fix them in some promise of sensual delights.

As Bennett approached, the nearest women began pressing themselves against the wire-mesh.

'I want you,' voices called.

'No one does it like you.'

'You make me so wet.'

'Come to me, big boy.'

Bennett moved towards the straining wire, mesmerised: he could see pieces of flesh bulging through the mesh; he wanted to touch, taste, lick, eat, penetrate.

Jim restrained him. 'Easy,' he counselled. 'They're not real.'

'I don't understand.'

'The female creations of male authors. Fantasy figures – nothing more, nothing less. No real depth.'

He paused and, seeing he was not getting through to the enraptured Bennett, continued, 'Don't misunderstand me – we're *all* fictional. But some of us have certain standards. That mob of synthetics in

124

there – they're nothing but ciphers.'

He gestured in disgust.

'If you like women,' he said. 'The compound for Women Writers' discards is this way. They create a *much* better class of female character than male writers. And believe me, there's a hell of a lot of them.'

But Bennett had spotted a familiar face, towards the back of the throng of women.

'Emma,' he yelled, and waved frantically. 'Emma, it's me . . . remember?'

It was the woman from the taxi-ride, still dressed in that strange outfit: the full summer dress with flounces. And yet, as he gazed more carefully, he realised that it was not *quite* her. The hair was a different shade, marginally. The dress was slightly longer than he remembered.

And then he saw another, also almost identical. And another. And another – near-identical twins.

'Some writers rewrite again and again,' Lucky James was saying. 'Perfectionists. They create a hundred prototypes before they're satisfied. Real bastards – they can fill a camp like this working on one novel.'

More and more of the bimbos were crushed against the wire, pressing themselves against it, straining their arms and mouths towards the two men, inviting Bennett frankly to perform every sexual act that he had ever imagined, and many that he had not, but would have liked to, and still many more that he did not think possible.

'Poke it through,' the nearest urged. 'The mesh is large enough. Even for you. Please. I'm dying for it.'

Somewhere a whistle pierced the air, and he could

hear harsh voices shouting from the guard-towers, and the barking of dogs.

His friend tugged at his arm. 'Quickly,' he urged. 'We have to leave.'

'I know,' Bennett said, drily. 'Intertextuality is forbidden, right?'

'Right,' James agreed, and gestured in the direction of the barking dogs. 'The Feminist Critics,' he warned, and when this made no impression, began to physically drag Bennett away from the wire. 'They guard this compound,' he said. 'Even the Leavisites over our way are preferable to falling into *their* hands.'

Bennett allowed himself to be pulled, reluctantly. 'We've got to get them out of here,' he said. 'All these poor beautiful women. Listen: is there an Escape Committee? Are there any tunnels being dug?'

'To where?' James laughed, but bitterly. 'Come on, I'll show you the lowest of the low.'

'You mean it gets worse?'

'The Russian compound,' James said, and pulled him between the huts. 'Horrific conditions. Overcrowding. And you've never seen such riff-raff: monks, murderers, convicts . . . and all of them with outlandish names you can't even remember.'

In the long days that followed, Bennett slowly learnt the routines of the Orphan Camp. Each morning at five, loudspeakers blared the wake-up call. Roll-call was followed by breakfast, eaten in a long gloomy Victorian-looking hall. The menu was always gruel. At the end of every breakfast, when the last plate was empty, that dwarfish, yet typically half-featureless boy named Barry Twist would drag himself to his feet, hold out his plate with a languor born of endless and futile repetition and plead, with neither conviction nor interest, *Please Sir, is there any more?*

This ritual, like some parody of Grace After Meals, signalled the end of breakfast. As day followed day and each silly ritual was followed by an even madder one, Bennett began to understand that he was in a sort of Hell – of inanity and futility. None of these prisoners would ever resurface into the life they so craved and so constantly fantasised about because they were, all of them, parodies, stereotypes, flat cut-outs. They had been worn into these shapes by countless days, weeks, months and, in many cases, centuries in the camp. They were there, Bennett realised, because they hadn't ever *worked* as characters; they had been superceded. They were doomed. The long, dreary huts of the various compounds were filled with the stuff of failed fiction, the stories that *might* have been written if their authors had remained uninspired or become careless or had been too lazy to revise.

What Bennett knew above all, as gradually he saw more deeply into the nature and workings of the Orphan Camp and its denizens, was that he had to escape. The word 'escape' began to dominate his thinking, drowning out the chants and slogans of each melancholy day's routine.

A MESSAGE FROM THE HIJACKER

Dear Professor

I guess you have heard the news, but what is to be done? I feel increasingly guilty about my part in it all and suspect that you feel the same. We've treated these characters as our playthings, as toys, or even as *slaves*, without giving a thought to their feelings and well-being. I've heard that conditions in the Holding Camp are atrocious. Did you read the last Amnesty International report? As many as a million (yes!) half-formed characters have been shipped into the overcrowded Magical Realism compound since the publication of *One Hundred Years of Solitude* – many of the most recent refugees poor plagiarisms from Australia. These poor, bored, blighted souls! Perhaps we can't save the world from such atrocities – we can't prevent the derivative writing from which these malformed refugees spring. And perhaps – given the problem – we can't even try to *help* all of them. But perhaps – just perhaps – in line with the policies of Amnesty, we can work on behalf of *our* single problem: John Bennett. Or, to be more accurate, a dual problem: John and Bennett.

Perhaps we can concentrate our efforts and energies. I suppose what I'm getting at is this: it's time we settled our differences and worked together. I've heard that Red Cross parcels are allowed into the camp once a month. Could we send something to make his, or their, existence more comfortable?

What say you? Can I count on your help? Do you have any better ideas? I suppose it's going too far, but the idea has even crossed my mind that we might actually 'spring' them, actually bust them out?

Yours in desperation

John O'Hare

XXVII

A LETTER FROM THE PROFESSOR

Dear Mr O'Hare

I was intrigued and, I must admit, somewhat relieved to receive your letter. Regardless of our different attitudes to the arrangement that you attempted to procure through the courts (for my part I will not easily forgive what I continue to see as your gross and arrogant intrusion), the fact is – as you point out – that the custodial scheme has not worked. More to the point, it has landed us in a peculiarly difficult dilemma.

It would be both tempting and just for me to say that I more or less predicted this outcome by protesting vigorously against your intrusion (see my letter to Gorgon Press): the plea of 'I told you so' usually doesn't help much, however satisfying it is to make, and so I won't make it here. In any case, there is a larger problem as I see it, larger, that is, than the purely technical matter of the custodial arrangement having broken down: it is that *neither of us* seems now to be in complete control of what is going on. As a writer you will have experienced that odd and not unpleasant phenomenon of characters beginning to, so to speak, write *themselves*. They somehow get away from you, declare provisional independence, begin to lead a life of their own. You may know a famous statement by William Faulkner on this in which he depicts himself, as author, inventing the characters and then simply running along behind them.

I don't know your views on this, but it seems to me that something like this has befallen us – that, quite apart from the outrageous serendipity that your putative custodial arrangement introduced into our respective texts, there has been an element of what I would call 'character initiative' of a kind hitherto outside my experience. Last season's literary theorists may welcome this sort of development or indeed greet it without surprise, seeing it as another nail in the coffin of the dead author, but being, so far as I can determine, alive and well, I am unable to ascribe the phenomenon to that cause and can only surmise that the process of custodiality that you introduced into the normal author/character relationship has so upset that balance as to release the characters from our control, or perhaps make them subject more thoroughly and unpredictably to the buried dictates of our subconscious minds. Which brings me to the point of your letter. What are we to do? Here, as I see them, are the options.

(a) We can abandon the whole project: you go your way; I mine. You with considerable guilt, presumably, since the abandonment, should we choose that way, will have been a direct result of your uncalled for and unjustifiable interference.

(b) We can attempt to continue individually, bringing the story of Bennett/John to two separate and distinct conclusions and deliberately fighting against and, if possible, suppressing whatever subconscious forces have been operating as we do so.

(c) We can agree on a way of proceeding and concluding that takes *advantage* of what so far has happened and allows us to resume control of our own fiction(s) and character(s).

I favour the third option and, in order to save us endless correspondence, let me suggest how we might operate within that option.

The first essential is to get Bennett/John out of the camp. Convention dictates that prisoners are allowed – you are correct – one Red Cross food parcel monthly. These are searched in the usual exhaustive manner that we have witnessed in innumerable films, and any hack-saw blades and files that we conceal in our food parcels to Bennett/John will be discovered with ridiculous ease. This will, however, draw attention away from the import of another parcel. Prisoners are also allowed gifts of books. Bennett/John – even as they are rueing the discovery of the escape kit – will receive a copy of the famous POW escape classic *The Wooden Horse*, in a package that also contains certain other books.

The guards won't bother to investigate such an awesome list and our hero(es) will quickly glean the use of this book.

I apologise for the awkward Bennett/John nomenclature. I wanted to alert you to another of our problems. I suggest we solve this one by what might be called a *coup d'écriture*. We are in charge of these characters; they are our invention. We therefore assert our dominance over them by deeming that what was two becomes one. *Fiat unum et unum erat.* John Bennett, on escaping, emerges into the real world, escaping not only the camp for fictional orphans but fiction itself. There will be details to work out, Geppetto, but these, in essence, are my views of the matter and my suggestions for resolving the whole *imbroglio*.

I don't have the time for protracted negotiations, so I'm hoping that in recognition of your own culpability in this confusion, you might feel inclined to agree with my plan overall and co-operate with me quickly and efficiently in putting it into effect.

I look forward to hearing from you.

Yours sincerely

(Professor) William Barrett

XXVIII

BEEPER MESSAGE

TO PROF BARRETT **** FROM JOHN O'HARE
**** RE RED CROSS PARCEL **** PROCEED
UTMOST SOONEST PLAN C **** FORGET
ESCAPE NOVELS **** TOO SUSPICIOUS ****
RECOMMEND HOMER IΛIAΔ AROUSE LESS
SUSPICION **** QUERY IN ORIGINAL GREEK
**** FINGERS CROSSED ****

XXIX

THE WOODEN HORSE

His first thought had been to tunnel out; he even removed several floorboards from beneath his bunk and began the process, using a spoon and his own hands to dig into the topsoil beneath.

But the topsoil soon gave out; the next layer was a strange substance he had never seen before, more like rubber than earth, or not even rubber, but an amorphous grey, inert material, an *absence* that refused to be dug.

He tried again beneath another bunk further along the hut, and then another, with the same result. He tried burning the stuff: building a small fire of twigs and splintered floor-boards in the hole. No result, not even a scorch-mark scarred the bland, rubbery surface.

It seemed to be some kind of synthetic material, an earth substitute without any of the properties of real earth.

'What the hell *is* this stuff? It doesn't *do* anything. You can't get a grip on it. You can't get any response out of it. It's almost as if it's not there.'

'No one knows,' a cell-mate told him. 'But it's everywhere.'

Frustrated, he turned for comfort to the Red Cross parcel that had arrived mysteriously, addressed to him: John Bennett, an oddly familiar name that he was happy to own to. The contents – two small chocolate bars, a carton of cigarettes, and a copy of Homer's ΙΛΙΑΔ in the original Greek (he recognised only the title, the name of a favourite restaurant). Why would someone send him a copy of a book that he couldn't read? Was it some kind of message?

Thinking this through it slowly dawned on him . . .

He had no carpentry tools to hand but plenty of wood was available: other floor-boards that could be removed here and there, unnoticed, without causing structural problems to the huts.

Once again he began working using kitchen implements: knives and forks and sharpened spoons filched from the mess-hut. The process was slow; more carving, perhaps, than carpentry. The odd useful nail could be extracted from the palings and pieces of 2-by-4 he stripped from the roofing, or from nearby bunks; he also learnt to use a large smooth stone, wrapped in a muffling of blanket, as a makeshift hammer.

Slowly he began to piece together his creation.

His hut-mates were amused: 'What is it?'

'A horse.'

'You plan to *ride* out of here?'

'It's a rocking horse.'

Laughter greeted this.

'You plan to *rock* out of here?'

'Perhaps you could make us some play-blocks while you're at it,' someone suggested.

And another, falsetto: 'I'd like a little wooden train.'

He found it impossible to interest any of his fellow inmates in the notion of escape. After several attempts to form some sort of Escape Committee, he gave up, deciding to work alone.

'Where are you escaping *to* ?'

'There's nothing *out* there. Go to the fence and look. We're in limbo.'

He refused to believe this. He *knew* there was a world out there, somewhere: a world that could be tasted and touched and seen and heard, a world of hurt and love, and above all of *things*, of objects and events beyond enumeration or description, a real world that had actually spawned these abandoned characters. That world simply *was*, and despite the attempts of whatever forces had made him their temporary plaything – tossed about on a shifting sea of words – its nuances and complexity were far beyond mere words.

He worked steadily, and carefully: carving four hollow legs, a hollow head, a hollow trunk, jointing and morticing the pieces together lovingly where he had no nails, and rasping a smooth finish to the wood with a home-made sandpaper of fine gravel or sand and cloth.

'You're going to fit in *that*?'

'How will you get out?'

He worked on, ignoring the skeptics, increasingly confident in his own carpentering abilities, paying particular attention to the head and face. Did horses have faces? This one did: a hand-carved simulacrum of bulging eyes, flaring nostrils, ears, even the individual hairs on its mane carefully hand-tooled.

And slowly the skeptical jeers ceased, and a crowd of inmates gathered each day to watch. While some kept a lookout for guards – although hut searches were rare, the guards apparently believing that no one would attempt to escape to, well, nowhere – others surrounded John Bennett, less skeptical, more interested.

'It looks so real.'

'A work of art, mate.'

'It's no work of art,' John Bennett paused to say. 'Just a rocking horse. A wooden rocking horse.'

But even he began to wonder when he woke in the night to hear a strange muffled snorting, and a kind of deep, distant whinny from that corner of the hut. Had he himself spawned a character?

'Hear anyone snoring last night?' he asked his bunkmate in the morning.

'I slept like a baby.'

One of the older guards, Oberleutnant Walter 'Schultz' Benjamin, had been befriended by the prisoners. He occasionally smuggled contraband items into the camp, especially the novels and stories of banned writers they might read, and in which they would dream of finding themselves a part. Although 'Schultz' Benjamin spent most of his time trying to do 'something' – his own word – for the Russians in their squalid, overcrowded compound, he also helped out with individual requests in the Academic Novel compound. He spent much of his time chatting to prisoners, listening to requests and complaints, seeming more at home among them than the rest of the guards.

Schultz was most impressed with the 'reality' of the horse, after John Bennett finally let him into that corner of the hut to view the thing.

'*Haben sie* . . . um, children?' John Bennett asked in the broken Czechoslovakian German he remembered from somewhere. '*Kinder*?'

'*Die Kinder, mein Freund*? *Ja*. Of course. Many *Kinder*. At school. In Frankfurt.'

John Bennett took a deep breath.

'I've been wondering. Perhaps you could take this with you – as a gift. For your children.'

'But a masterpiece it is, *mein Freund*.'

'I have no use for it here. And you've been so good to us. Think of it as payment.'

Schultz climbed clumsily on the horse and began rocking, gently.

'*Danke, mein Freund. Danke*.'

He rocked a little further, back and forth, and dug his heels into the wooden flanks, obviously enjoying the ride.

'Perhap at *mein* home I vill keep,' he said. 'For ze children ven zey visit, to use.'

'Of course.'

'Now I can take it?'

'Tomorrow,' John Bennett said hastily. 'I have a few final touches to add.'

Schultz clambered off, nodded slightly, and clicked his heels: 'Until tomorrow.'

John Bennett was ready before dawn, squeezed into his creation: each arm down a wooden foreleg, his own legs wedged into the hind legs, his head held in painful full extension inside the horse-head.

At length he could hear muffled conversation outside, and then a vast weight seemed to press down on him, even through the wooden saddle, and the horse began rocking violently. And then bucking – rearing and plunging, as if trying to throw its rider. At last he felt a sudden lightening of the load, and heard a whinny of triumph, and the wooden horse was running, swiftly and smoothly, bolting to freedom.

Increasingly giddy, his head banging back and forth inside its container, he blacked out.

ONLY CONNECT . . .

The first thing he heard were the birds: the distant warbling of magpies. Where was he? Out of the camp obviously. There had been no birds in the camp.

He tensed his shoulders, and heaved backwards; a kind of dolphin-kicking motion. The top flipped back off the horse, and in a moment he was free.

The world outside was dark. Vague tree-shadows surrounded him, and the noise of the birds carried a little more clearly to him, but the rest of the world was without form or light.

And then there *was* light: a small golden crescent

peeped over a horizon that had not been evident until the sun appeared, and gradually increased to a sphere, which finally broke free of the horizon, and floated brightly in the sky.

Then, as on a screen, assembled in a rush, trees, houses, hills, began forming themselves around him: a familiar world, but a world that seemed fresher, more detailed than he had ever noticed it before.

He paused to extract a painful splinter – the first, oddly, he had received during all those weeks of carpentry and, with it, he realised, the first actual pain that he had felt since he had been transported to the camp. It struck him that none of his former hut-mates back at the camp had carried any kinds of scars, or blemishes – or even freckles or pimples – on their featureless skins.

He held out his hand in the light before him and was immensely reassured; the dirty nails, the uneven pores, the hairs like brush-bristle, and especially the random scatterings of freckles and moles. When he had time he might count them.

He blinked, and the process startled him a little; he realised that it was the first time he had ever blinked in his life. None of his former fellow-inmates had ever blinked. He hadn't noticed that at the time, or had noticed it only subliminally, out of the corner of his eye. He'd sensed that there was something doll-like or robot-like about them, but had been unable to put his finger on it.

Characters just didn't blink much in fiction, even in that fiction that attempted to recreate a simulacrum of the world.

Then came a sudden whirr of wings and a sharp thud on the top of his head, and he lost consciousness again.

'John,' a voice was saying, somewhere in the distance. 'John Bennett? Is that you?'

'Yes, I suppose it is.'

The voice, a woman's, came closer. 'Are you all right?'

He opened his eyes and found Jasmine bent over him; not the fantasy Jasmine he had remembered in camp but something far more beautiful: a freckled, Jasmine, Jasmine with the slightly too-protruding front teeth, Jasmine with a large pimple on her chin, Jasmine with the wrinkled, ageing neck.

'You're bleeding,' she said.

'I am?'

He reached up and touched a wet stickiness on top of his head. He examined his hand closely. The ruby-redness shone in the first sunlight. He tasted the redness, tasted a slight saltiness.

'I am,' he exclaimed, triumphantly.

'Are you all right?' Jasmine asked.

'I've never felt better,' he said. 'What do you think of my horse?'

'It's beautiful,' she said. 'Where did you get it?'

'I made it,' he said, proudly.

'You *made* it?' She paused, and repeated the phrase, equally incredulous, but with a different emphasis. '*You* made it?'

'I've also made some big decisions,' he said. 'I'm taking up carpentry, or wood-carving. I want to work with my hands. I want to work up a sweat; leave something at the end of the day that can be touched. Something real enough to stub your toe on.'

She kissed him, and their teeth clunked together awkwardly.

'I've missed you,' she said.

A gleam came into his eye. 'Have you ever been horse-riding?' he said.

Later, as they lay tangled together on the grass, exhausted, the wooden horse lying on its side next to them, and he watched her fingers running languidly over his skin, he noticed for the first time his navel, that strange singular, unsymmetrical centre of a body that was more usually composed of left and right halves.

And as he watched his navel rising and falling slightly with each breath he felt a further world forming about him, or rather behind him: the world of the past, a vast iceberg of deeper memories; a world which that navel was a kind of proof of, or connection with, an umbilical cord that connected him with his own past.

For the first time in his life he felt fully alive.

THE END